Other Side of the Wormhole

Book 1: Switched

Celia Mai

Dragon's Den Publishing, Inc.

This book is a work of fiction. Names, characters, places and incidents are either the product of the author's imagination or are used fictitiously. Any resemblance to persons living or dead, businesses, events or locales is coincidental.

No part of this publication may be reproduced, distributed, or transmitted in any form or by any means, including photocopying, recording, or other electronic or mechanical methods, without the prior written permission of the publisher, except in the case of brief quotations embodied in critical reviews and certain other noncommercial uses permitted by copyright law.

Dragon's Den Books
Published by Dragon's Den Publishing, Inc.
Dragon's Den Publishing, P.O. Box 10441, Gulfport, MS 39503, U.S.A.
Copyright © Celia Mai 2013
All rights reserved
ISBN 978-0-9890257-0-6
Text set in Times New Roman
Printed in the United States of America
The publisher does not have any control over and does not assume any responsibility for author or third party websites or their content.

*For Karen, Matt and Amanda.
Thanks for being my guinea pigs.*

OTHER SIDE OF THE WORMHOLE
Book 1: ¡Switched!

¡Switched!

CHAPTER 1

Daphne was screaming. Her fingers clawed at the concrete support column. The moment she lifted into the air, she reached out for something to hold on to. The white concrete stood between her and her father, who had his legs wrapped around it for leverage. She felt her father's grip on her wrists beginning to give. He dug his fingernails into her flesh in a last ditch effort to hold on. Her ears were still ringing from the explosion that had caused the roof of the mall's food court to cave in.

"Please," she breathed, her voice barely above a whisper, "don't let go."

Around her, tables and chairs had been scattered, overturned by the blast. There was still a cloud of dust in the air. Debris littered the large area. Rain should have been streaming in through the hole in the middle of the roof. Instead, it was held at bay by the strange blue light surrounding the strange man who'd descended.

The initial panic had passed and the mad scramble for cover was over. People were huddled trying desperately not to be seen. Aside from her own panicked voice, she could hear a jumble of voices saying, "Oh God! What the hell is that?" coming from all directions. For half a second, she thought she could see someone taking video with a cell phone.

Finally, her grip was wrenched free and her father's hold broke. His fingernails left bloody cuts in her wrists as she was torn away from him by some unseen force. Flailing and still screaming, she flipped through the air until her back landed against the man's chest. He wrapped his arm around her neck, locking her in a loose choke hold. She did her best to struggle, but he merely tightened the grip with his arm, decreasing her air supply.

Daphne felt her stomach lurch. The world below her seemed bathed in an eerie blue light. Wait, she thought, below? She was overcome by terror as the damaged tile floors shrank away. They passed upward through the gaping hole in the roof toward the sky. Held firmly in the man's grip, she watched helplessly as the buildings below dropped away and became invisible, replaced by layers of clouds and an endless expanse of sky.

She expected to be dragged into the black vacuum of space where she would suffocate or have her body turned inside out by the lack of atmosphere. Or maybe at the last second, they would disintegrate into thousands of tiny particles and rematerialize onboard some strange alien ship. Or better yet, this was just some horridly vivid nightmare. Instead, the blue light melted into a shimmering aurora.

Steele relaxed his grip on Daphne as they glided down the beam of light toward the forest floor. He set her down gently and watched as she staggered and then dropped to her knees beside a tree. Her body shuddered as she retched repeatedly. Steele did his best to conceal the fact that his own knees felt like jelly.

He hadn't made a portal jump in over a decade and thanks to her, he'd made two within the past 30 days. His organs were still trembling and he felt like his insides would never stabilize again. Steele crossed his arms to hide his shaking and leaned against a tree for support. He didn't want to take the risk that any sign of weakness on his part would give his quarry a chance to escape.

To Daphne it felt as if she was tumbling from the sky. She dropped like a sack of potatoes beside a tree and proceeded to lose her lunch. She wrapped her arms around the trunk of the tree for support and gasped for breath. She wiped her tongue on the sleeve of her sweater to try and clear the bad taste from her mouth. She had to let saliva build up in her mouth before she spat to clear away the dust from the explosion and tiny strands of sweater lint. "This is all just a bad dream," she tried to tell herself. But the pain in her wrists told her that wasn't the case. Her wrists still ached from where her father had tried to hold onto her and she was still bleeding a little.

Steele sauntered toward her. If Daphne hadn't already been trembling from the urge to puke again, she would have been trembling with fear. He grabbed her roughly by the back of her collar and jerked her to her feet. That motion really made her want to throw up again. In one swift motion, he slapped a pair of glowing handcuffs on her and let her drop back to the thick grass covered ground. Quickly, she turned her head to the side and heaved.

Steele retreated to a tree about four feet away. He crossed his arms and watched as she took in her surroundings. She seemed to be mumbling to herself.

"You may as well forget it," he said. The statement got her attention. She stopped muttering and briefly made eye contact with him.

"Forget what?" she asked.

"Whatever spell you're trying to cast," he said, furrowing his eyebrows at her. The corners of her eyes squished together while her eyebrows went up. Her lips were parted slightly as her mouth turned partly into a frown. She looked at him in disbelief.

"I wasn't…are you," she paused. She was about to call him crazy, but was suddenly aware that insulting her kidnapper would only make a bad situation worse. She was, after all, at his mercy.

"Crazy?" He finished the question for her. She shrugged. He flashed what could only be described as a sinister smile. "No, and I'm not stupid either." After a pause, he spoke again. The smile was gone. "Those are magic handcuffs. Go ahead. Try and finish that spell and see what happens."

He seemed to be daring her to try something. "I wasn't casting a spell." She wanted to say it with a little bit of bitterness and sarcasm, but the words squeaked out giving away the level of her terror. "I was making mental notes."

"About?"

"This," Daphne said, gesturing to the forest with her head. If the chance presented itself, she planned to escape and try to find her way home.

"If you're thinking about escaping back to that little planet you were hiding on, you can forget that too." He snapped.

"Why would you say that?" She had wanted to ask nonchalantly, but something about the way all his comments sounded like threats caused the words to rush from her in a panic. He didn't answer. She waited as patiently as she could, her anxiety growing. When she couldn't take it anymore she asked again. "Tell me. Why did you say that? What are you going to do with me?"

He pushed his body away from the tree and a small black notebook appeared in his hands. There was no flash of light or weird chanting. Daphne blinked several times. Maybe he had pulled it from a secret pocket somewhere. Her time to ponder the mystery of the black book quickly vanished as he approached her. Instinctively, Daphne scrambled backward. There wasn't really anywhere for her to go. She was trapped by trees and her hands were bound.

"I'm going to put you on trial."

"What!"

Steele stopped directly in front of her and took an official looking posture. "Diamara Katz, you are charged with the following: possession of stolen property, inter-dimensional travel without a permit, criminal use of magic and murder."

"You've got to be kidding." Daphne protested. Steele's face told her the charges weren't a joke. "This is ridiculous. I knew it. You are crazy."

"Do you confirm that you are Diamara Katz?"

"What?"

"Are you—"

"Yeah, I heard you the first time." He cocked his head slightly to the left and raised one eyebrow. "No." she snapped. "I'm not her."

"Then what alias do you assume?"

"Alias? I don't have an alias. My name is Daphne. Daphne Morrow, not Diamora or whatever."

Steele made a note in the little black book before continuing. "Let the record show that the prisoner denies the aforementioned identity." He paused and looked at her with cold eyes. "Normally, you have the right to a limited use of magic. Should you abuse that right, your powers will be fully suspended until your hearing. You have the right to legal representation. If you cannot afford a defense… that is unfortunate. Please verify that you have heard and understand."

Daphne's mouth couldn't help but drop open. The rights were a far cry from the Miranda rights she had come to know so well from years of watching Law and Order on television. And just what had he meant by 'normally'?

"Please verify that you have heard and understand."

She shook her head. "This doesn't make sense. What about the right to remain silent? Or innocent until proven guilty? You make it sound like I'm on my way to death row already."

Steele shrugged. "It's what you deserve."

"Now wait a minute." She struggled to rise to her feet. It was difficult with her hands tied.

"Please confirm that you have heard and understand!"

"I heard you and I understand the charges and my rights. Is that what you want to hear? But I'm telling you, you've got it wrong. I'm not who you think I am." He stared at her with cold, disbelieving eyes. "I'm not a murderer!"

"That's for the Sages to decide."

CHAPTER 2

Steele allowed her a few more minutes to protest before he finally grew tired of watching her flounder around on the forest floor. He hauled her up by the collar of her sweater. The material was soft and shifted easily forcing him to twist it in his hand to maintain his grip. It was a pullover sweater and the twisting and lifting action caused the girl to gag as he forced her to her feet. The action served two purposes. As the sweater pressed against the front of her neck, it partially choked her, causing her to stop talking; and it quickly reminded Daphne that he had complete control over her and her situation.

Daphne tried to rub her sore neck but her injured and bound wrists made the action difficult. Plus, she didn't want to give this man any reason to think that she was trying to use 'magic' to escape. She studied the bully who stood before her. He towered above her. She was only 5'4" and he was at least a foot and a half taller than her. It was dark in the forest so she could be misjudging his height. From the moment he'd put her in the choke hold, she could tell he was fit. His whole body was a mass of carefully chiseled muscles. His mind was probably pretty sharp as well. Timing an escape might be impossible.

It was too dark to see his eye color or any fine details of his facial features. To do this job, he couldn't be very old. He was probably in his early to mid-thirties. His hair was short, but long enough that it shifted when he moved. And for a kidnapper, he had a melodic and alluring voice. He was probably quite the ladies' man, she reasoned.

As much as she was studying him, Steele was studying her. He'd spotted her a few hours before he made his move. She was much shorter and younger looking than the reports suggested. She should have been about 5'9", in her mid-thirties, and sporting tattoos between the joints of each of her fingers. But those features weren't anything that a simple magical illusion couldn't alter. Despite the slight dissimilarities, she looked exactly like her wanted poster: light caramel skin, dark brown curly hair and green eyes. She was dressed a little outlandishly, but he figured that the clothes were necessary to fit in on the planet where she'd been hiding.

Satisfied that he'd given himself more than enough time to recover from their journey, Steele turned the girl toward the thicker part of the forest.

"Walk or I'll drag you." He gently shoved her and she shuffled her feet forward.

Daphne allowed herself to be half dragged through the forest as the man did his best to keep her in front of him. The pain in her wrists had died down to a dull throb. Some of the cuts were starting to itch and she really wished she could wash and bandage them properly. Since she was a bit of a germaphobe, tramping through unfamiliar woods with branches and leaves rubbing against her only made her nervous that the cuts would get infected. Besides that, she was still covered in dirt from the explosion at the mall.

"Can I ask you something?" she said, panting. The man didn't respond. After a brief pause, she asked anyway. "What's your name?"

"My what?"

"Your name?" she asked again, this time shouting over her shoulder. "You do have a name don't you?"

"Yeah. I've got a name."

"Well?"

"Why do you want to know?"

"You know my name and apparently a thousand other names that you think I've used. It seems only fair that I know who you are."

Steele chewed on the inside of his cheek as he thought about it. He didn't usually give his name to the people he was assigned to. It usually wasn't necessary. His reputation tended to precede him. He simply tracked them down, handed them over to the Templar and collected his bounty. *I guess there's no harm in it*, he thought.

"Steele," he said.

"Do you have a last name?" Silence. That was something he definitely wasn't going to answer.

"Steele huh? That doesn't sound like a real name. More like a code name or something," Daphne ventured. She'd hit the nail on the head but Steele kept quiet. "So Steele, why did you kidnap me and where are you taking me?"

Steele let out an involuntary snort, the audacity of this woman to accuse him of kidnapping! She really sounded like she believed it too. It was probably all just part of her act to throw him off guard. Either way, he didn't like the allegation hanging in the air. He wanted to keep things straight about who was the villain.

"I didn't kidnap you," he snapped. "I arrested you and I'm taking you to the Sages for trial."

"Why would you need to arrest me? You're obviously an alien from a planet with superior technology that considers me to be some inferior life form. I'm from a planet in the middle of nowhere. There's no way I could ever have made it to wherever here is to commit any crimes, let alone murder."

"I'm not an alien and you may as well put a sock in it. I'm not falling for it. You're just a murderer who jumped bail and traveled illegally to an alternate dimension."

"So officer, does that mean your people give you the authority to just go wherever you want and kidnap young girls who are shopping with their parents? I mean, don't you at least have a point where your authority ends?"

"If I was one of the Templar maybe. But I'm not an officer," he said rudely, giving her a rough shove. "And for your information, you gave me the right to use any means necessary to bring you back when you skipped town and made that illegal portal jump."

"So," Daphne mused out loud, "Steele's a bounty hunter. Then that must make these Templar people he mentioned something like the police?" She put that last statement in the form of a question on purpose. She hoped it would draw conversation out of him without her having to ask directly.

"If you think they'll be inclined to listen to your lies, trust me, they won't be. Not after you killed six of them the first time you tried to escape."

"Does the whole world have a grudge against this woman?"

"Not this woman…you."

"But I'm not—"

"Still denying it I see." He shook his head and ticked his tongue.

"Look. I'm no scientist, but you had to cross into an alternate dimension to catch me. So isn't it possible that you got the wrong me?"

"Possibly, but highly unlikely."

"Isn't there some way to tell?" Daphne pressed. "Like DNA?"

"DNA's no good," Steele said matter-of-factly. "It always matches or it's close enough that the Templar tend to overlook the discrepancy."

"What about fingerprints?"

"Same thing."

"How about my quantum signature?" Daphne almost laughed at herself once the words were out of her mouth. Now she was pulling ideas out of her butt.

"Quantum Signature?" Steele said it like a question but he really seemed to be considering what she'd said.

"Sure," Daphne said, trying to sound confident. "I've seen enough Sci-Fi shows to know that my universe and your universe exist on different planes or wavelengths or, well, you know what I'm trying to say." He nodded. Since he was walking behind and to the left of her, Daphne was able to glance over her shoulder and catch the tail end of a nod. "So there should be a way of checking to see if you got the wrong me then, right?"

"I suppose," Steele said with a shrug. "But I don't have the equipment or the authority for something like that."

"Oh. Then who does?"

"The Sages."

"Then maybe—"

Steele cut her off mid-sentence. "Don't count on it."

"But—"

"You said so yourself," he reminded her. "It's guilty until proven innocent. You're name's already on a very short list."

Daphne's shoulders sank. He had paraphrased what she meant, but he was right. There was no way she was going to get a fair trial. Even if there was some way to prove she wasn't the person they were looking for, powerful people don't like the world seeing them make mistakes. Nothing was more damaging. It was one thing to be an incompetent leader. It was another thing to be seen being an incompetent leader. They would torture her or execute her to satisfy the masses and sweep any other evidence under the rug. At 15, it seemed her luck and her lifeline had run out.

CHAPTER 3

Daphne counted her steps to give her mind something to do. Steele had stopped answering her questions or supplying indignant grunts to her comments. Unnerved by the strange sounds of the forest, she counted her steps in her head and had attempted to keep track of how many times he turned her left or right. Unfortunately, she had lost count of how many times she had lost count.

The thickness of the forest ebbed and flowed like the tide. Just when it seemed they would be crushed by the jaws of nature, the foliage would begin to thin out and the remnants of a path would appear beneath Daphne's feet. Thanks to her horrible sense of direction, she had quickly lost track of which direction they were headed or how long they had been walking.

Flashes of fine silvery light played on the ground near her feet. Daphne glanced up. Was that moonlight? Or maybe it was merely some alien glow worm or firefly or just her mind playing tricks. It was so dark she had given up trying to see anything in front of her and instead relied completely on Steele's guidance. Her chances of escape had vanished with the sunlight. Steele roughly shoved her head down. Her forehead just barely missed colliding with a low hanging branch while her cheek was kissed by the budding thorns of a vine.

"Isn't there an actual path to wherever you're taking me?" Daphne snapped. She quickly brushed away the leaves and pushed strands of her now wild hair out of her face.

"As if I'd give you the satisfaction," he mumbled. She would have rolled her eyes if she thought he would have noticed or cared.

"I get the feeling you've used this path of yours a lot," Daphne said sarcastically. He shoved her head out of the way of another branch and into yet another tangle of thorny vines. "Please, I think I'd prefer the concussion."

Steele snorted. He had kept her walking around in circles for the past five hours. The Templar had given him the job of finding her for them, but they couldn't be bothered to show up on time. He would rather have waited at the rendezvous point, but knew that if he sat around letting her study the forest and that if she somehow managed to escape, the Sages would have his head. Steele gazed up through an opening in the canopy overhead. Had he blinked he would have missed the three rapid flashes of crimson light. There was a brief pause followed by three more flashes of light.

"It's about time." He breathed a sigh of relief and turned Daphne slightly to the right. "Let's go."

Daphne felt her intestines knot. She winced. The pain was worse than cramps. "How could I have been so stupid?" she thought. "This whole time we've been going in circles. I could have run."

She barely staggered a few steps paces before the trees ended and the world fell away. She gasped as the loose ground gave way beneath her. Daphne screamed as her butt slid across the ground and her feet met empty air. Steele quickly grabbed her belt and pulled her back onto solid ground. She was panting and trembling, the sound of her own pounding heart echoing inside her head.

"Are you alright?" His own palms were sweating. He alternated the hand holding her while he wiped his hands on his pants.

"Yeah. Thanks."

"Try to stay alive for the next few seconds. I don't get paid if I don't deliver a live product."

Daphne was uncertain of what to say. It was good manners to thank someone who'd just saved your life, but Steele's comment made her wish she could take the words back. After all, he was the reason she was in this mess. It would have been better if he'd just let her fall.

Daphne shuddered. "Don't think like that," she told herself. "There's still a chance this will all work out and you can go home." It was a slim chance, but still a chance.

Daphne finally took stock of her surroundings. Behind her was a thick, black wall of trees. Before her was the edge of the cliff she'd almost fallen from. The forest was dense. There was no way to tell how big it really was. She and Steele were standing on a small patch of dirt. There were rocks and a couple of tufts of half dead grass. If she craned her neck to look over the cliff edge, she could view the world spreading out beneath them. It was like looking down at Atlanta from a hotel window at night. The city lights went on forever. Traffic flowed in all directions, glittering like multicolored Christmas lights.

Above her, the sky glowed with the light of the moons. Daphne rubbed her eyes and blinked to make sure she wasn't imagining it. They dominated the sky, like miniature planets, each casting a different colored light on the world below. One, which hung lowest in the sky, was a silvery gray marble. The sight of it made her home sick for the night sky of her own planet. The other was an ethereal blue. Both appeared to be a hair's breath away from collision. Of course, she knew enough science to know that they were hundreds of thousands of miles apart.

At this altitude she felt she was close enough to reach out and touch the satellites of heaven. The view was majestic. Daphne loved nature and normally would have been mesmerized by the breathtaking scenery around her. Unfortunately, her present situation made it impossible for her to do anything other than pray.

A cold wind rushed around her and she felt her body swaying from the force. She dug her heels into the sparse ground. Now that she was aware of the drop, she wanted to keep a safe distance from the edge. In the corner of her left eye, she saw a flash of red light. Then she heard it: the whistling of helicopter propellers? The wind picked up even more speed. Daphne was thrown of balance and bumped into Steele's shoulder. He took a firm hold on her with one hand and stood at attention, tightly gripping the black book in the other.

They stood together and watched the craft descend from the sky. For Steele, each moment brought with it an increased feeling of relief, while Daphne trembled with growing dread. Everything Steele had said rushed to the front of her mind. He was turning her over to the Templar. And they thought she had killed six of them in an effort to escape. Cop killers on Earth were hated by both the police and the average citizen. It was safe to assume the sentiment would be the same here. She should count herself lucky if she even made it to face trial by the Sages.

    The ship looked like a long rectangle with wing-like extensions just behind the starboard and port bows. The same wing-like devices were just before the starboard and port quarters. Two sets of glowing blue lights were on the underside of each of the wings. As the ship descended, Daphne could see that the ship was constructed of thousands of interconnected hexagons. It parked a few feet away from the cliff, hovering in midair. Six triangular sections of one of the starboard walls opened up and a gangplank extended toward them. Daphne gasped and took a step back.

    Ten men exited in a two by two formation, positioning themselves around her and Steele. They were all tall, slender and muscular. Every uniform was perfectly tailored to fit. Each wore a dark cape, and a helmet which only left the eyes, nose and mouth exposed. Tucked into a belt at the waist, was a sword on one side and a gun on the other. Another man exited the ship. He had to be the commanding officer.

His uniform was more ornate than the others. He wore a heavy black cape and his shoulders were adorned with epaulettes. He had about six medals pinned to either side of his breast. Like the others, he wore gloves, except his were white instead of black and had brass studs across the knuckles. He approached them and Daphne almost took another step back.

"Don't move," she told herself. "They might…no," she thought, "They definitely will take it the wrong way." Daphne lowered her eyes and avoided making direct eye contact with any of the Templar. These men looked more like soldiers than police.

"Good work," the officer said. His lips parted in a self-satisfied smile.

"Hmn." Steele grunted.

The officer took the extended black book from Steele's hand and read over the contents. The engines stirred dust into the air. Daphne glanced up and quickly looked down at her feet again. She drew air in between clenched teeth. Her body swayed and the ground had started to spin. The man's face had a scar running from the jugular vein in his neck, up his face, over one eye and stopping at the tip of his forehead. The eye with the scar was artificial. It had been replaced by a colored mechanical eye which reacted to the shifting shadows around them just like a normal eye would.

"Go ahead, stare if you want," he said. "I don't mind if you admire your handiwork." His voice dripped malice.

"Oh God," she thought, her breathing coming in shallow gasps. "This is it. I'm going to die."

"Look!" As if compelled by magic, Daphne's head snapped up. She could feel her eyes pinned wide by her own fear. She wanted to blink, anything to break his gaze, but her brain seemed to have forgotten how. She stared at the leathery skin of his sun aged face. He swung a massive gloved fist at her and she cringed. The man laughed.

"Witch!" He swept her feet out from under her. Daphne fell backward onto the ground. He kicked her in the stomach. She coughed as the wind was knocked out of her.

"Not so tough without your magic are you." He tried to spit in her face, but missed the mark. Instead the liquid landed in Daphne's hair.

"Hey," Steele cut in. "Until you pay, she belongs to me. I'll thank you not to damage my merchandise." Steele looked down at Daphne. Tears had begun to pool in the corners of her eyes. A solitary tear escaped her right eye. It left a muddy streak and settled in the crease around her nostril.

"What's your rush bounty hunter? From what I hear, you're owed a little payback of your own. Go ahead. I promise not to see anything."

"I'll get my justice in court, now…" Steele rubbed the tips of his already outstretched fingers together. The commander pulled a small metal rod from his pocket and waved it over the pages of the book. He closed the book and handed it back to Steele. On top of it was a glittering prism shaped crystal.

"Pleasure doing business with you." Steele gave the man a hasty two-finger salute and vanished.

"Get this piece of filth on the ship. Make sure she's locked up with triple guards," the commander ordered.

"Sir, yes sir!" the soldiers said in unison. One of the soldiers lifted Daphne up by the handcuffs and practically dragged her across the metal gangplank. She willed her legs to move, but fear and uncertainty had sapped all the energy from them.

CHAPTER 4

Daphne was thrown aboard the ship.

"Ah!" Before her eyes had a chance to adjust to the lighting, she was shoved against a wall and frisked. It was worse than the TSA's modified pat down. The soldiers' hands groped her in areas even she rarely touched. Her solar powered watch was snatched from her wrist. Daphne cringed as she heard the mother of pearl clasp snap. The rose gold cross her mother had given her for her birthday was roughly removed. She was thankful it had come with a magnetic fastener.

Her pockets were turned inside out. Loose change clattered to the floor and she could hear the rustling of paper as a soldier counted the dollar bills she had left over from her shopping spree at the mall.

"What's this?" One of the soldiers removed her mp3 player from her back pocket and turned her around. Daphne squinted in the dark. The soldier held the device in front of her. It was small, about four inches long and three inches wide. She shivered from the cold feeling of the wall against her rear.

"It's my mp3 player," she croaked.

"A what now?"

"It plays music."

"Well, you won't be needing this where you're going."

"And where exactly am I going?" Daphne's voice shook. She was glad it was too dark to see. Not being able to see the fury in this man's eyes was the only thing keeping her from peeing in her pants. He loosened his grip on her and turned away. Daphne felt herself relax a little.

She felt his fist before she even saw his shadowy figure move. Without warning, the soldier turned and punched her. For a moment, Daphne saw stars. Colored flashing dots took over her field of vision. She raised a hand to cup her bleeding lip, but the soldier pushed it away. Daphne's heart slammed against the inside of her chest. Tears stung her eyes. A rush of warm air flowed around them as the triangles closed into a hexagonal shape.

For a brief moment, they were plunged into complete darkness. Beams of silver light instantly lit the area. Strips of light curved around the base of the ceilings and floors. Overhead strips of light were spaced approximately 6 feet apart to provide extra light. Daphne's eyes struggled to adjust to the sudden shift in brightness. Her vision was still blurry from the blow to her face. Five of the soldiers had positioned themselves in front of the sealed door. If she hadn't just seen it close, she would have mistaken it for part of the wall.

"Move!" the soldier who'd hit her gave her a shove. As Daphne attempted a step, the soldier kicked the back of her knee, knocking her off balance. She fell onto the cold metal floor. He kicked her in the ribs several times before roughly dragging her up by the collar of her sweater. He continued to abuse her as he guided her through the twists and turns of the narrow hallway.

The glowing front wall of the cell vanished just long enough for Daphne to be thrown in. Her right shoulder hit the metal floor first. Her lip ached and she could taste the saltiness of her own blood. Already she could feel her left eye beginning to swell shut. She coughed up a bitter tasting liquid and tried to spit to clear the taste from her mouth. Even the slightest movement of her lips made the pain worse. Her ribs and stomach ached, and the muscles in her thighs and back throbbed.

Daphne groaned as she curled into the fetal position. She watched as the glowing wall reappeared. The translucent wall of light was all that separated her from her captors. Daphne was suddenly sleepy. The floor spun beneath her. Blotches of black and gray crept into her field of vision. She blinked and they quickly faded, yet returned a few moments later.

"Looks like she has a concussion," a voice said. Daphne blinked. She raised her hands to block out the bright light, but they wouldn't move. She tried again and again before her panic subsided enough for her to realize they were restrained behind her. Where was she? What was going on?

"Bhuren certainly did a number on her," the voice continued. The light switched off and she felt herself being lifted into a sitting position. She blinked several times and tried to clear the fuzziness from her mind. The darkness she had been battling had begun to subside.

"Well, what do you expect," someone else said. "She murdered his brother. If it had been me, I can't say she'd even be alive right now."

"Murder?" Daphne murmured. "What murder?" Daphne's tongue tasted the words. Her mind felt like it was made of strawberry slushy.

"Are you done pretending?" the second voice asked. "Are you ready to confess your sins and accept the Sages' justice?"

The words were more effective than throwing cold water on her face. Daphne's mind quickly replayed the incident at the mall and her time in the forest with Steele. In an instant, she relieved the explosion which had collapsed the food court roof and thrown her backwards from her chair. For a brief moment, her wrists throbbed where her father's fingernails had dug in in an effort to hold onto her. She shuddered as she recalled her brush with death when she'd almost stepped off the edge of a cliff.

Even though it was the most recent, she couldn't remember much of her time with the soldiers, except that they'd given her a thorough beating. Her head was pounding. She tried to reach up and rub her temples, but her hands wouldn't move.

"Handcuffs," she slurred. When had they shifted the handcuffs behind her back? Had she fallen asleep, or simply lost consciousness?

"They moved them after you passed out," the first voice said. Daphne blinked and looked into the man's face. Her vision was still a little hazy, but she was beginning to see his features clearly. He had pointy ears, pale skin, and thick black eyebrows. He flashed a smile. His teeth were mostly white but were beginning to brown with coffee stains. His head was topped with a mountain of black curls and his chin and cheeks had a layer of black and gray studded stubble growing. He was kneeling beside her

"Who are you?" she asked.

"Dr. Onmiouji, but my friends call me Ouji." His breath was thick with the odor of coffee and something stronger. The smell made Daphne a little sick to her stomach.

"And of course," the second voice chimed in. Daphne looked in the voice's direction, but didn't see anyone there. "We all know who you are. Though I never thought I'd find myself face to face with the greatest evil sorceress the three worlds has ever seen. Diamara Katz. It's a wonder you even got the chance to escape the first time."

"Daphne."

"Excuse me."

"Daphne. My name is Daphne. Daphne Morrow."

"Still playing at that are we?"

"Bacchus, that's enough. You're no longer needed." Dr. Ouji snapped.

The force field door flashed off and then on again. Daphne turned her attention back the doctor. He wore the same uniform as the other soldiers, except he didn't have a belt. He had taken off his gloves and laid them beside a steel case. His cape was white with thin purple trim instead of black. The case lay open and Daphne could see a collection of small metal tools.

"Are those your weapons?" she asked.

"I'm a doctor. I don't carry weapons."

"But you're one of them."

"Doctors don't have to carry weapons if they don't want to. I don't consider them necessary for my profession."

"Why are you helping me? Don't you think I'm some sort of dangerous criminal?"

"You're wearing the handcuffs, so I'm pretty sure I'm safe. Here." He held a steel tumbler to her lips. Daphne jerked her head away.

"What is it?"

"Water."

"How do I know its water?"

He poured some of the clear liquid into the palm of his hand and then drank it. "See? Water."

"How can I be sure it's water and not recycled sweat or truth serum or something like that?"

The man laughed. "You watch too much Tech."

Daphne frowned. "How can I be sure this isn't some kind of trick? You know they beat me and then send you in to befriend me and I tell you all my secrets?"

"Do you have any secrets?"

That's a stupid question, Daphne thought. Everybody has secrets.

"No," she told him. He smiled and winked before offering up the cup again. She let him hold it to her mouth. She took slow, delicate sips. It was clear and cold. It had a faintly sweet taste, like that of a fresh juicy apple.

"How is it?"

"It's good."

"I'd offer you some food, but if I treat you too much like a person, it'll just make things worse for you." He gestured his head in the direction of the cell door. Daphne could make out the vague figures of about three soldiers.

"Just how many of them are there?"

He chuckled. "If you're planning on trying to escape, don't. We're too high up. Besides, you'd never get away with it a second time."

"You're just like them, aren't you?" she asked. "You think I'm her. You really think I did all the horrible things Steele said?"

He shrugged. "You can't argue with the evidence."

"What evidence? What proof does anyone have that I'm guilty?"

He shrugged again. "I don't know. And even if I did, I couldn't tell you."

"That's just great."

"But what I can tell you is they've got orders to kill you if you so much as look at them the wrong way."

"I'm not from this planet. How am I supposed to know which way's wrong?"

"Just look at your feet and don't speak."

"Dr., I really don't know what's going on here, or how I got into this mess. I just want to go home." Daphne's voice broke. She cleared her throat and blinked back tears with her one good eye. The doctor didn't react. He just stared at her with a neutral expression on his face.

"What's going to happen to me?"

"If you're really innocent, it's probably better if you don't know." He rose to his feet, gathered his belongings and left.

CHAPTER 5

Daphne stretched her legs and looked around. It was like being in an oven, minus the glowing metal coils on the roof and floor. The room was a shiny gray box almost completely devoid of furniture. There was a thin metal shelf protruding from the back wall. Beside it was something that resembled a sink. The floor had been polished so well it reflected everything.

Daphne looked down at her reflection. She could smell the strong scent of antiseptic. Tiny bandages had been placed on the small cuts on her cheeks and collar bone. Her swollen eye and mouth didn't really hurt anymore. There was a purplish sheen to them. The doctor must have put some sort of medicine on them. She didn't have much feeling in her lip or her eye. It was as if they had been injected with Novocain. Her injured eye twitched slightly when she blinked. The doctor had stitched her busted, swollen lip and even though they were tied behind her, if she flexed her wrists, the skin felt sticky, as if super glue had dried on her skin. It feels like liquid bandage, she thought.

Daphne shifted her body the best she could in an effort to find a comfortable position. She tried sitting cross-legged, stretched them out again, and finally settled on bringing her knees up to her chest. She wanted to lie down, but the effort of leaning sent waves of pain shooting through her ribs. Gasping and blinking back tears, Daphne thought about trying to stand. Unfortunately, for that action, her sore abs would have to do all the work.

She was curious about the translucent, glowing wall. The force field was the only thing separating her from the soldiers on the other side. The milky colored barrier made it impossible for her to see the faces of the men guarding her. She could faintly make out passing shadows. If I scoot closer and squint with my good eye, she thought, I could maybe count them.

"This is ridiculous," she mumbled to herself. "I don't know where I am or how anything works and I'm trying to plan an escape. I wonder if my parents would think I was crazy or stupid if I just sat here and let them kill me, or if they'd want me to try and get out of here?"

"Be quiet in there!" The voice was distinctly female. The soldier approached the force field. Daphne could tell the woman had her hands poised above her waist.

"Sorry, I just wanted to ask a question." She lied, the idea of escape still at the front of her mind.

"What?"

"Are you right handed or left handed?"

"Handed? What the frell is that supposed to mean?"

"You know, do you use your right arm or your left?"

"They warned me you play mind games."

"I think it's a perfectly valid question."

"Fine. I'm multisided."

"Multi...sided?"

"Don't get any ideas. It means I can use one side just as well as the other."

"You're making that up."

"Maybe so, maybe not. Care to test me?" She paused, then let out a cynical chuckle. "I thought not."

As the soldier stepped away from the doorway and regained her post, Daphne sighed. So much for escaping, she thought miserably. I suppose I should just give up on it and see how it plays out, Daphne rationalized. There's too much I don't know about this place. Anything I do will just make the situation worse. If I go to court, there's a chance I can get out of this mess. No. If I leave my life in their hands, I'm as good as dead. Tears sprang to her eyes. She couldn't blink them back or wipe them away.

"Well doctor," the commander said, "what's your professional opinion?"

The commander had his feet propped up on the end of the conference table. Between his teeth was an Endzian cigar. The leaves and herbs rolled inside usually gave off a faint scent of citrus and the smoke was pale blue. The casing was white with gold scroll designs. This particular cigar produced gray-blue smoke and a smell like burning hair: a sign that the cigars had been taken apart, filled with illegal substances purchased on the black market, then rolled again. Whoever sold these had taken care to match the seams in the designs.

The commander's cape hung from a peg on the wall and his gloves had been tossed haphazardly on the wet bar beside the door. His area of the table had six empty shot glasses which were carefully stacked end to end to form a tower. In his left hand was a tiny glass containing a dark brown liquid.

Sitting on the commander's right was Steele. The bounty hunter tried his best to look bored as he nursed a glass of the same dark drink as the commander. The table was populated with a collection of soldiers, doctors, and scientists. Across from Steele was Bhuren. Sitting at the opposite head of the table was a representative of the Sages.

The representative was dressed in black robes edged in sparking silver satin. She wore a hood which hung so low it almost obscured her nose. She sat with her hands tucked inside her sleeves. The woman didn't seem to breathe. Despite her tight fitting clothes, her chest didn't seem to rise or fall. Every movement she made was so delicate that, if not for her jingling jewelry, he wouldn't have known she was alive. To the untrained eye, the woman could have been mistaken for a statue, or Death himself. If the lights were off, her clothing would allow her to virtually disappear.

Doctor Ouji pursed his lips. He frowned as he watched the commander swirl the fluid in his glass. It was against regulations to drink during a shift. The doctor placed a small crystal on the table and waved his fingers slowly above it. The lights in the room darkened and a hologram appeared above the table. The image was split into three parts. On the far left was a picture and profile of Diamara Katz, on the far right was a picture and profile of Daphne, and the center was blank.

"Well, to be perfectly honest…" he cleared his throat before continuing. "There are three possibilities. While each is equally likely, I think there are two which are far more likely than the other."

"Oh frell!" the commander snapped, finishing his drink and slamming the empty shot glass on the table. "Quit being vauge and just get on with it."

"The first theory, which is, of course, the most popular opinion, is that the person we have in custody is in fact Diamara Katz. The second theory is that this young girl is telling the truth."

"Preposterous," the commander snapped. He waved a hand in the air as if to physically brush away the idea. Doctor Ouji cut a hateful glance in the commander's direction.

"It's people like you that made this whole process necessary in the first place."

"Please doctor," the Sage's representative cut in, "continue."

"There are too many minor things to ignore between this Daphne person and the sorceress Katz. Daphne is missing not one, but every single magical tattoo and artifact that Diamara possessed."

"Tattoos can be removed and jewels can be taken off and hidden," a female soldier chimed.

"Their finger prints are very similar, however, there are enough slight differences to make me doubt."

"Again, someone skilled in black magic could easily change things like that."

"But—" the doctor tried to argue.

"I think that the young Templar has a point doctor," the Sage's representative spoke. Her voice was eerie, yet melodic. "Please, skip over anything trivial. Height, eye color, and things of that nature are easily manipulated by one skilled in the dark arts. It is how the sorceress was able to be granted bail in the first place. Using a disguise and an alias, she easily fooled the Templar and the Court into letting her go. By the time her deception was discovered, it was too late. They cornered her, but the magic handcuffs had already been removed and she brutally murdered several honorable men and women in order to escape."

Dr. Ouji sighed. He continued, "As chief scientist and physician for the realm of Capytal, I have studied the tissue samples of both Diamara and Daphne. There is a significant age difference between the two."

"Doctor," the Sage's rep urged, "I thought we had made our position clear on the physical dissimilarities."

"Yes, of course. I apologize. Um, I should warn you, the girl has sustained some injuries."

"Nothing serious I hope? The Sages would never require an injured person to stand trial." Dr. Ouji fought the urge to roll is eyes at an obviously hypocritical statement.

"Oh, it's nothing for your owner to worry about," the commander sneered. "She just got a few bruises during the portal jump. It seems our bounty hunter here has slippery fingers. He must have dropped her."

Steel frowned, but kept his mouth shut. It was a mistake for anyone to get on the wrong side of any member of the Templar, especially the one in charge of dividing assignments among the guilds and signing the pay orders.

"The doctor patched her right up, didn't you Ouji?"

"Yes. She should be fine in a few days. Uh, while the girl was unconscious, I did search her memories and found no trace of any magical knowledge, knowledge of this dimension, or of the criminal exploits of Diamara Katz. All her memories consist of those of Daphne Morrow of the planet Earth."

"Interesting," the Sages representative muttered. "What do you suppose this means?"

"Well, since anyone refuses to entertain my theory that this girl is who she says she is, the only other idea is that she suffers from Portae Languorem." The middle section of the hologram lit up. In the picture was one body colored red and another, colored green.

"What the frell are you talking about?" the commander croaked as he downed another shot of alcohol.

"Portae Languorem or Portal Sickness, as it is more commonly known, is a condition where someone from one universe can switch minds with someone from another. Essentially, the person's body is the same while her consciousness is different." The doctor waved his pointer finger and the brains from the green and red pictures switched places.

"So what you're telling me," the commander slurred, "is that because she has the body of the sorceress, but the mind of some kid from another dimension and the sorceress is in this kid's body?"

"Precisely."

"That presents the Sages with a unique dilemma," the representative said softly.

"I don't see a problem," Bhuren rose to his feet so fast his chair flipped back and clattered against the floor. He slammed his palms on the table as he raged. "The Sages should just kill them both!"

"If they have switched brains as the doctor suggests," Steele interjected calmly, "then killing this girl doesn't solve the problem. Katz is still out there with a younger body and free range in a dimension that is millennia behind in technology and magical knowledge. Unchecked, she stands to become the most powerful person in that dimension and any other where she can gain a foothold."

"This is the most ridiculous—"

"Bhuren, that's enough." The representative countered. "I must contact the Sages. They will need time to consider the options before she goes to trial."

"I won't let that demon escape justice." Bhuren drew his sword as he headed for the door. He froze mid-step. His face contorted in agony. The sword dropped from his trembling fingers and clattered to the floor. The metal vibrated briefly, letting out a shrill, almost musical sound.

"And just where do you think you're going?"

Bhuren choked and groaned in agony. He slowly dropped to the floor. He lay on his side trembling. His eyes slightly glazed over with a yellowish haze. No one moved to help him. Many of the Templar rubbed the hilts of their swords underneath the table, but focused their eyes on the long oval tabletop. The commander stepped over Bhuren's twitching body to pour himself another drink and grab a fresh cigar.

"Do you think you are the only one who deserves justice in this matter? It is the Sages' duty to consider the issue at hand and provide judgment. Not yours."

Dr. Ouji loudly cleared his throat. "Your grace," he said, raising his head to meet the representative's gaze, "I think you've made your point."

"Of course." The Sage's representative smiled briefly in his direction. On the surface, the smile was confident and satisfied.

However, Ouji could sense the fear behind the woman's eyes. "Far be it from me to argue with someone of your stature."

Her hidden jewelry jingled ominously. Ouji felt the hairs on his arms stand on end. Bhuren's twitching ceased and the yellow coloring began to fade. Bhuren gasped heavily for air. His body was still shaking. Ouji gestured to the Templar. Two soldiers on Steele's side of the table quickly rose. One grabbed the man's sword with one hand and helped lift him with the other. Together, they carried Bhuren from the room.

"And Commander, don't let me catch you allowing the abuse of our prisoners again," the representative barked.

"I never—"

"Please, don't insult my ability by trying to lie. Men like you have never been good at it, or much of anything for that matter."

The commander muttered a curse under his breath. Even Steele, who was sitting closest to him, couldn't make out the words. The representative snapped her head up. The hood fluttered away from her face momentarily to reveal glowing red eyes. When she spoke, her voice had lost the icy melody and been replaced by a raspy, almost acidic sound.

"Don't forget, you can easily be replaced."

CHAPTER 6

Addison's left arm hung limply at her side. She lifted her wrist and jingled the handcuff chain against the table leg. She shook her head and cradled her forehead in her right hand and rubbed her temples with the tips of her fingers. Addison leaned back in the uncomfortable metal chair and stared at the wall. She knew that it was really a one way mirror. The agents were probably standing on the other side watching her and discussing their next strategic move.

The room was one of many interrogation rooms she'd seen over the past several days. Some were larger than others. This one was probably the smallest. It was about the size of a half bathroom with a cheap metal table and chairs taking up the majority of the space. She was surrounded by pale gray cinderblock walls and sealed in behind a heavy steel door. Each time an interrogator came and went, they would lock the door behind them. Her ears had come to hate the sound of jingling keys and clicking locks in the same way most other people hated the sound of nails on a chalkboard.

"Mrs. Morrow," the female agent said as she entered the room, "would you like some coffee?"

"I don't drink coffee."

The agent shrugged and laid the extra paper cup on the table along with a napkin and a paper plate full of donuts. She pulled out a chair on the opposite side of the table and eased herself into it. The agent's joints popped. Her fake smile accentuated the laugh lines around her mouth and the crow's feet in the corners of her eyes. She switched her coffee cup to the opposite hand and took a long sip.

"Mrs. Morrow, do you know why I'm here?"

"I'm not stupid. They think if they send a woman in here that I'll just start confessing to whatever it is they think I did. Ha. Fat chance."

"So, does that mean you have something to confess?"

"Nope."

"Mrs. Morrow, I can help you."

"How? Are you gonna find my daughter? Are you gonna bring Daphne back to me?"

"It's obvious you and your husband were involved in a terrorist conspiracy and Daphne was just an innocent victim in all this. Maybe it didn't start out that way, or maybe you acted under duress to protect your daughter from harm. Just tell us what you know and we can help you. I can get you a deal."

"Listen lady…I'll tell you exactly what I told those other agents. We didn't do anything. We don't know anything. I don't know who or what that man was. I don't know if it was human or alien or whatever. And frankly, I don't care." Addison blinked back tears. "All I know is that thing has my daughter and while you people are treating me and my husband like criminals, you're wasting the time you could be spending looking for her."

"Ma'am, the United States Government does not acknowledge the existence of extraterrestrial life. We're working under the assumption that this was a test of new technology by a foreign power."

"If that were true, then why would these people take Daphne? We're not rich."

"No, you're not. Our investigation has revealed some very interesting details about your personal finances."

"So you think we turned traitor to pay our mortage?"

The agent shrugged. "Why don't you tell me."

"This is ridiculous. I want a lawyer."

"You do know we have the right to hold you for 72 hours without charging you."

"That's funny because it's been almost 4 days and you still haven't charge me with anything. You've repeatedly denied my request for an attorney, you won't let me make a phone call and you're keeping me here against my will. You won't tell me where my husband is, you're violating my rights, and breaking the law."

"We're just doing our job."

"Well I think you're all failing miserably."

"I'm curious, just what do you think our job is?"

"To investigate what happened, to find the truth."

"Well we have reason to believe you and those closest to you know more about what happened at that mall and your daughter's disappearance than you're leading us to believe."

"Either charge me or let me go."

"This was all just a plan to cover up a murder so you could claim the insurance you have on her, wasn't it?"

"You're insane. If you knew what it took for us to have Daphne and how much we love her, you wouldn't think that, not even for a minute."

The agent just smiled and took another sip of her coffee. "Alright. Let's say, for a moment, that I believe Daphne was abducted by aliens. What exactly would you expect us to do about that?"

"I thought the U.S. Government didn't acknowledge the existence of aliens."

"Humor me. If in fact your daughter was taken by intelligent beings from another planet, what do you think we could do? Just how do you expect us to find her and bring her back? Assuming she's even still alive?"

Addison's mind went blank. She looked from the cold metal table to the wall behind the agent's head and back at the agent. She shook her head.

"I don't know." Her voice cracked. She tried to clear her throat, but the next words were barely audible. "I honestly don't know."

Hot tears burned her eyes. Her vision blurred. She gasped for breath between sobs. "I just want my daughter back."

"Believe me, I want the same thing. Just tell me what you know about the country or countries behind this. Tell me how you and your family got involved. Tell me everything you know about this new technology and I promise you, we'll do everything in our power to bring your daughter back."

"I can't."

"Mrs. Morrow, this deal won't be on the table forever."

"I can't tell you what you want to know, because I don't know anything."

There was a quiet knock on the door. The agent rose to her feet. "Excuse me." She closed the door quietly behind her and stepped into the hall. Two men in darks suits were waiting for her. Each had a white I.D. tag clipped to the left side of his lapel. The fluorescent lights cast a bluish glow on the white linoleum floors and the white walls. Both men were senior agents to her. She recognized Agent Wilson; he was her direct superior, but she had never seen the other man before.

"Why did you stop me? I think I was close to breaking her."

"Agent Parks, this is Agent Johnston. His unit will be taking over the case."

"On whose authority, if I may ask?"

"That's classified," the agent replied coldly.

"What department are you with?" Parks asked.

"That's classified."

"I'm sorry Parks," her boss said, "but Johnston's clearance exceeds ours. We have to cut them loose."

"What? Why?"

"The official statement is that those two have lawyered up and are refusing to cooperate with the investigation."

"Impossible. They haven't had access to a phone and they've been under 24 hour surveillance. How could they—"

"It seems the husband's brother's son is a lawyer. He saw the video on the news, called the son and the two of them have been making a scene with the media. You know, calling the government tyrannical, accusing us of breaking the law, violating civil rights, the whole nine yards. Not to mention pushing this as an obvious alien abduction. We have no choice. Cut 'em loose."

"Aliens, seriously? Sir you don't—"

Johnston held up a hand to silence her. "President's orders. I wouldn't worry. We've got wire taps in place, IT has gone through every computer, we have phone records, text messages, financials—if they so much as sneeze, we'll know." He made no effort to smile or even make eye contact.

Agent Parks sighed and pushed open the door. Isn't this just great, she thought bitterly. The first case I get to do something other than shuttle papers around and I was on it for less than 3 minutes. Of course, this wasn't the first time she'd been pushed off an investigation because her clearance level was too low.

'Classified' was really just a more sophisticated way of saying, "None of your f-ing business."

Addison looked up at her with red, swollen eyes. Parks fished a ring of keys out of her pocket and unlocked the handcuffs. She watched as Mrs. Morrow stared at her wrist in disbelief. She was clearly confused. She started to stand and sat down, yet kept her knees and feet poised to spring up at a moment's notice. She reminded Parks of a rabbit.

"You're free to go."

"I don't understand."

"You can go home, but I wouldn't leave town. I'm sure we'll have more questions for you."

Addison Morrow stood, steadying herself against the cheap metal chair. What was going on here? Being granted her freedom should have brought a feeling of relief. Instead, it only intensified her fear and panic about Daphne.

"Agent Johnston will show you out," she said, gesturing to the agent who had swooped in to steal her case. "You can collect your belongings at the main desk."

CHAPTER 7

Emory stared out the car window. His eyes took in the landscape as it transitioned from crowded metropolis to open highway, and finally to two lane country roads. His brain never registered the difference. The hours that passed felt like seconds to him. Rain drops slapped against the windows and the sound of the windshield wipers echoed in the silence. The water dripped down the tinted window and pooled in the tiny exterior window sill.

Addison sat next to him with her chin balanced on her palm and her forehead pressed against the glass. Her other hand lay limply in her lap. Neither of them had spoken since being released from interrogation. Her head bounced up and down as she quietly drifted in and out of sleep. He smiled to himself as he remembered Daphne's head nodding the same way on long car trips. No matter how she tried, Daphne couldn't manage to keep her eyes open. It's amazing how alike those two are, he thought. They both drool from the left side of their mouths and toss and turn in bed. He chuckled as he remembered a sleeping Daphne at six months old, waking him from a nap by kicking him in the head after he'd fallen asleep with her tiny body on his chest.

"At least she's not making that God awful noise," he said to himself.

He was referring to Addison's habit of grinding her teeth. Whenever she was stressed or upset, she would do it, unknowingly of course. Whether she was asleep or awake, she would grind her teeth together until she felt the issue had been resolved. Daphne, on the other hand, snored. Her snoring was a soft, rhythmic purring like noise. Unlike her mother's teeth grinding habit, Daphne's snoring was sporadic. This shopping trip had been one of the first times he'd heard that snore in years. Ever since she'd gotten too big to be tucked in, there hadn't been many opportunities to watch his angel sleep. Now that Daphne was gone, he wondered if he would ever have that chance again?

"Stop it uncle Em," Galen said from the driver's seat.

"Huh?"

"I know what you're thinking. You're worried about Daphne. Where she is and what's happening to her and if you'll ever see her again. But you can't start thinking in what-if's. We don't know anything yet. Have faith."

"Easier said than done." He glanced over at Addison. Her head nodded and eventually her other hand dropped into her lap and the seatbelt was left to support her neck on its own. She sighed.

"I never thought I'd feel like a crazy man. When they asked me what I thought happened, you know what I said?"

"What?"

"Aliens. The word came out of my mouth before I even realized I said it. I said aliens and they laughed at me."

"Can you blame them?"

"Hell, I would've laughed at me too. But they weren't there. They didn't see what happened. They weren't holding onto her when she was snatched away, ripped from my own hands like I'd been holding on to her with cheap toilet paper."

"Uncle—"

"You know Daphne always loved that science fiction stuff. She would always ask me, what if this and what if that? I humored her of course, but me, I never believed in any of it until now. Until—" He couldn't finish the sentence. He shook his head and went back to staring out the window. Addison slipped her hand into his and squeezed. Her eyes were still closed.

"You just leave everything to me. I'll do what I can to clear this mess up," Galen said.

"No one can fix this," Addison said, her voice faltering. She squeezed her closed eyes firmly. Gasping, she took several deep breaths. Her body shook and she clenched and unclenched her fingers. Emory undid his seatbelt and slid closer to his wife. He pulled her close to him and let her head rest on his chest. As he kissed the top of her head, his vision blurred and warm tears streaked down his face. He closed his eyes, but the tears continued to flow. He lacked the will to stop them.

The media had already taken up residence across the street from their house. News vans were cluttered together on every available patch of dirt and grass. Like vultures feasting on a carcass, the reporters crowded in the center of the road. Galen donned a pair of sun glasses to help block out the flashes from the cameras. He was glad his firm had allowed him to tint the side windows of the company sedan extra dark. At least the press would have to wait until his aunt and uncle got out of the car before they could photograph them in their moment of misery.

The private security he'd hired was fighting to keep the media correspondents from blocking the driveway and off the family's property. The sound of tires crunching gravel was drowned out by the jumbled shouts of reporters. Galen turned onto the driveway and put the car in park. He removed the sunglasses, tucked them inside his jacket and quickly got out to face the press. He left the driver door slightly ajar so Emory and Addison could hear his speech. He'd been practicing it in his head for the majority of the 10 hour drive.

"As attorney and representative for the Morrow family, let me just say that these accusations of terrorism are preposterous and completely unfounded. There are hundreds of eyewitnesses and video evidence to prove that this situation is beyond the capabilities and knowledge of a lower middle class family."

"Then you do believe that this was in fact an alien abduction?" a male reporter shouted? He'd come as close to the car as space would allow and was pinned in a self-imposed headlock as he attempted to squeeze past two overly muscled men.

"At this time, I'm saying that the era of scapegoat's and government conspiracies is over. All my clients' want is the truth and to have their daughter returned safely. Thank you."

He slipped back into the car and sped up the short driveway and parked in front of the door. Thanks to the security, there was no chance of the media trying to push their boundaries and creep onto the family's lawn. He looked over his shoulder and made sure his aunt and uncle made eye contact before he spoke.

"Get out and get in the house as fast as you can. Keep your heads down. Don't look at the cameras. If you do, you'll feel compelled to say something, to try and explain your side of things. Don't."

They nodded in understanding.

"Good. Dad's already in the house, so let's go." He shut off the engine and pushed a button. The power locks clicked off. For a few moments, Addison sat there frozen, her hands and knees trembling. She took several deep breaths, trying to steady her nerves. Before she was ready, Emory pulled her from the car. He put her in front of him and pushed her up the front steps. The front door opened just wide enough for them to squeeze through. Dylan closed and locked it behind them.

The inside of the house was dim. The blinds were closed and new curtains had been hung over every window. The curtains were thick and dark. Addison could tell Dylan, Emory's brother, had picked them out. The curtains didn't match anything and varied in length. Even with all the lights on, the place felt dark and closed in. Dylan had the television on, but he'd turned the volume so low that the sounds it produced were unintelligible.

She ran her hand along the back of the new pleather sofa to keep herself busy. If she didn't find something to do soon, she would lose her resolve and peek out the window. The last thing she needed was the media replaying the video of her peering from her own house like a crook in a hostage situation. Galen shed his jacket and tie, and found a place on the couch. He slowly flipped through the channels, pausing briefly at each news station to take in the footage before moving on.

"Geez," he snapped. "You'd think there wasn't anything else going on in the world. Every channel's either playing video from the mall or live coverage of your front yard."

Addison sighed. "I need chocolate. Daph, you want to split a bowl of ice cream with me?" Addison let out a cynical laugh as she looked into Emory's strained face. "Force of habit I guess."

"I don't think the world will stop if you fudge your diet a little."

"No. I guess not." She headed for the kitchen, stopped midway and turned back toward the living room. "I'm not hungry anymore." Without Daphne, her urge to eat anything was quickly vanishing.

"Addie—" Emory breathed.

"It's just not the same. Without her…I miss the way she'd always race to the kitchen so she could claim the caramel sauce and the way she'd always give me the dirty spoon if she accidently dropped one on the floor and how she'd always get bigger scoops for herself and finish off more than half the bowl." Addison didn't have to hold back tears this time. She didn't have any left in her.

"Why don't you two go get some rest? Galen and I can handle things." Dylan offered.

"I'm not tired," Emory muttered. "But Addie, you go ahead."

Addison's weary legs carried her up the stairs. She tried to avoid looking into Daphne's room, but the feds had made that impossible. They'd left her door wide open. As Addison moved to close the door, she froze. Her sorrow and despair quickly turned to fury.

"It's empty," she breathed. Screaming, she flew down the stairs. Emory leapt to his feet and grabbed her, barely stopping her from opening the front door. Her fingertips scraped against the brass colored door knob.

"What is it? What's the matter?"

"I knew they searched the place. They showed me pictures and they brought stuff in and out of the room, but her room? How could they? Why would they? Daphne's innocent! She didn't do anything wrong."

"It's my fault," Emory whispered.

"What?" Addison pushed him away. "Why? What on Earth would possess you to do a thing like that?"

"They were calling us terrorists. They accused us of any and everything you could imagine, and then they started accusing Daphne. I got angry. I told them they could take whatever they wanted and I dared them to find proof of so much as a parking ticket."

"I have parking tickets," Addison snapped.

"The point is, they're not going to find anything. The sooner they realize that, the sooner they stop accusing us and start looking for her."

"These people will make up evidence. Do you think the American people can maintain confidence in a government that would admit to being defenseless against little green men? And what do we do if she really was taken by aliens?"

"And what if she was taken by the government and all this alien stuff is just a cover-up?"

"That's insane."

"No more crazy than saying my daughter was snatched by E.T."

"What would they want with our daughter? Why Daphne? Why not someone else? And if it was the government, why make it a public spectacle?"

"I don't know."

"Because it's stupid! It doesn't make good sense! You—"

"That's enough." Dylan cut in. "Both of you just need to calm down. You're gonna make yourselves crazy. It's best to just try and put it out of your mind for the time being. Arguing about it and attacking each other isn't going to bring Daphne back."

"Well what do you suggest we do?" Addison barked. "I can't go through Daphne's clothes with her and help her decide what to wear for her first day of 10th grade, I can't call anyone because the phones are probably tapped. I can't go outside to get the paper because the press is camped three feet from my front door. I'm a prisoner in my own house. My daughter was taken from me and they've branded me an enemy of the state. We can't afford security and Galen's services for long. It all seems so hopeless."

"I know it's frustrating," Emory said, trying to sound self-assured, "but we'll figure it out."

"Not tonight you won't," Dylan chimed in. He handed Addison a fresh cup of hot chocolate. "I know you don't like coffee."

"Thank you." Addison gracefully accepted the cup. Her hands trembled as her mind played through all the different uses for the steaming liquid. She could drink it or open the door and hurl it at the news vans parked outside. Instead, she took a deep breath and breathed in the scent of double dark chocolate and marshmallows.

"This definitely tops being released from interrogation." She said, gesturing with the red ceramic mug.

Galen laughed. The outburst was sudden. It cracked through the room like lightening. "You only say that because you haven't tasted it yet."

"I didn't make it from scratch you know," Dylan said in his defense. "It came from one of those little packets."

"I wouldn't Aunt Addie. He can't even make a box cake mix taste good." Galen was laughing so hard, tears were running down his face.

"It's not that funny," Dylan snapped. He shoved Galen off the couch and planted his own rear end where his son had been sitting.

"Sorry dad. I was just thinking about the time you tried to make Daphne a cake for her birthday. It looked alright on the outside, but the look on her face when she bit into that cupcake…priceless." His laughter died away and his smile vanished. Addison followed his gaze. His eyes were locked on a picture on top of the piano. It was a picture of Daphne. In it she was about six or seven years old. Her curly hair had been pulled into two buns. She was standing on the deck of a boat wearing a green sweatshirt that said: Nessie Exists.

The picture had been taken about six months after Galen had graduated from law school. He'd saved his paychecks and convinced them to let him take Daphne to Ireland for an early Christmas present. Even then she'd been obsessed with stories of the impossible, so Galen treated her to a detour to Scotland. They'd spent two days riding up and down the loch, trying to catch a glimpse of the fabled Loch Ness Monster. Even though they weren't lucky enough to see anything resembling a sea monster,

Daphne couldn't be argued with. She was certain Nessie was down there and had been watching her.

For a moment, Galen held the picture. He cleaned the dust off with his sleeve and carefully put it back on the piano. "I've got some money saved—"

"Galen, don't," Addison spoke, shaking her head.

"I was saving it for, well, it doesn't matter. I want you to have it. Use it for whatever you need to help bring Daphne back."

"Galen," Emory's voice cracked. He cleared his throat, but his voice still wavered. "We can't take your money. We appreciate the gesture, but you're young and you still have your future ahead of you."

"I won't take no for an answer." They nodded and he flashed a weak smile. "Good. So dad, what's to eat?"

Dylan shuffled toward the kitchen. He wasn't hungry, but he needed to hide his face from his family. He didn't want them to see any evidence of the disturbing thoughts he was having on his face. He didn't want to accept or believe it, but Daphne being taken by aliens was fast becoming a very real possibility. They could spend every penny they had and it would all be wasted. If it was true, then it would mean that humans weren't alone in the universe. It would mean that the police would wash their hands of this and future kidnappings, chalking them up to alien abduction. And it would mean that any chance of finding Daphne and ever seeing his niece again would fade away like stars at dawn.

CHAPTER 8

Portal jumping cases were always more complicated than Steele liked. Every case involved inquiries and seemingly endless amounts of paperwork. From the moment he'd handed the sorceress over, he was transported aboard the ship and confined to a small, windowless room. There he'd been subjected to mind probes, magical scans and a battery of tests by Dr. Ouji. He could have done without the doctor's overly thorough medical examination, but it too was required, otherwise he could spend months locked in quarantine.

When asked, he provided the solicitor soldier with a written and signed account of his trip to Dimension .835 and finally, after a few more hours of sensory deprivation, he'd been assigned a room in the hunter's lodge. On paper, the word 'lodge' gave the place an air of sophistication. In reality, it was more like a cargo hold which had been converted into makeshift barracks. The males' rooms were made to sleep 10 comfortably while the females' rooms could sleep eight. Typically, a greedy starship captain would squeeze in seven extra people to maximize his government bonus for providing hunter services.

Steele lay in his bunk with his back to the other bounty hunters. This particular room had been designed to hold 14. Fortunately, for this trip he was only sharing the room with seven others. Counting himself, four were milling about in the barracks while the others had gone to trade gossip with the Templar soldiers or gawk at the latest captures.

He faced the wall and did his best to be as still as possible. One of the hunters bunking with him was Whisp. Whisp was a member of a rival guild and well known for being notoriously nosey. His code name was just a shortened version of 'Whisperer', his real alias. Whisp didn't usually take on subjects. He dealt mostly in information. How accurate and thorough his Intel was depended heavily on the price you were willing to pay.

Steele resisted the urge to look in Whisp's general direction. The other thing the man was a master of was drawing people into a labyrinth conversation. It was a unique technique he'd developed to help him steal secrets. The conversation would always seem harmless enough, but if Whisp walked away smiling, it was certain you'd said something you shouldn't have. Steele knew the trick well. He too had been caught in Whisp's web. The information hunter knew his craft so well that it could take you three days to realize you'd let something slip. Of course, if he did it right, a person could go an entire lifetime and never know he hadn't held his tongue. Steele ground his teeth in frustration. He'd allowed himself to fall victim to Whisp on more than one occasion.

Steele worked hard to keep his breathing even and his back straight. Resting on his mattress was a small round metal disk. The mini holographic projector allowed him portable access to his personal subject records. He used his body to block the other hunters' view of the light reflecting off the metal walls. He stifled a yawn and went back to his search.

Portae Languorem. The first time Steele heard those words was more than 30 years ago. If memory served, it was a single sentence blurb in the bounty hunter training manual. The last time he made a portal jump, the subject had tried to use Portal Sickness as his defense. Unfortunately for him, the Sage's hadn't ruled in his favor. That ruling, coupled with the corrupt nature of the Templar system had been the reason Steele had spent the last decade refusing portal jump incidents. He'd only accepted this case because he'd received a direct order from Guild Master Hyron.

After about five minutes of searching, he came across the record he was looking for. Since he made it a habit of ignoring names, all he had to go on was a vague memory of the man's face. Jonnie Hollum's digitized image stared back at him. A chill crawled up his spine and he couldn't control his body; he shuddered visibly. He scanned his signed statement to the solicitor and read through the medical report. All the physical stuff was an exact match: DNA, fingerprints, eyes, height, and etcetera. Jonnie's quantum signature matched their dimension, but his temporal readings suggested he was from another reality. That tiny irregularity wasn't enough to save him.

Back then, there weren't council meetings for evaluating the evidence, so things were often overlooked or purposefully ignored. Even with the council review, Steele thought, facts are still ignored. Oh well, cynicism doesn't pay and neither does activism. I've done my duty. It's up to them to decide what to do with her. If she's worth saving, fate will intervene.

"You don't really think that, do you Steele?" Whisp asked.

"This fish isn't biting." Steele shut off the hologram and tucked the metal disk in his pocket.

"Can't we just have a friendly conversation?" Steele rolled over to face Whisp. The other hunters had slipped out of the room sometime during his file search.

"There's no such thing with you."

"I'll bet you were looking through your files again. Probably wondering what will happen to that young sorceress you brought in. I'll bet you were thinking about old Jonnie what's his face."

Steele fought to keep his breathing even and his mouth shut. He's just baiting you, he thought. Most of what he thinks he knows is just guesses. It's how I respond that gives it away.

"You're only half right." Whisp continued. "It's part guess work. People don't realize that what they don't say tells me just as much, if not more than if they'd just open their mouth. Of course, you've always been easy to read. You try to act heartless, but you're not Cinnamon. You're far too invested in your cases."

"Mind your own business Whisp!" Steele gritted his teeth and swung his legs over the bedside. The worn soles of his boots thudded against the metal floor with force as he rose to his feet.

"Oh Steele," Whisp flashed a mischievous smile, "must you be so dramatic? If you don't want to be caught in my web, learn to block psychic magic." Whisp chuckled. "I believe that's in the training book too. Page one I think."

Steele tousled his own hair in frustration. "I need a drink."

He exited the barracks and stormed to the right. He walked for about five minutes before he realized he'd gone in the opposite direction of the ship's hostelry. Steele growled as his temper flared. He'd just given Whisp confirmation of whatever the meddlesome man was thinking. He sighed and started to pivot in the right direction. He stopped.

I'm only a few feet away from the holding cells, he reasoned. And there's a transporter pad on the other side of the guard station. I might as well keep going. It's already too late to change Whisp's mind or alter whatever it is he thinks he knows.

Steele slowed his pace and slowly approached the prison zone. The security was overwhelming. There was a check point with five heavily armored Templar placed six feet away from the security doors. He showed his hunter I.D., tucked the pendant back inside his shirt, and was about to move on when one of the soldiers placed a heavy hand against his chest.

"I didn't say you could pass hunter." The soldier spat out the last word with obvious contempt.

"Was there something else?" he asked calmly.

"Wait."

"For what?"

Steele didn't have to wait long for his answer. The five soldiers guarding the checkpoint were joined by five others. The squadron leader for the new collection of men and women exchanged a few hushed words with the current squad leader. He watched as glowing security keys changed hands. He was forced to wait as one by one the soldiers exchanged places. As the first squadron left, he attempted to pass, but was stopped again.

"I.D." the woman snapped.

"I just showed it to the other guy."

"I know."

"Then why—"

"In case you haven't heard, there are dangerous fugitives aboard. Now, your clearance card or you can turn around and go back to your room."

Steele sighed. He knelt down and fished his wallet out of a hidden pocket in his pant leg. He produced a glowing yellow card about the size of his thumb. The soldier waved a small metal rod over it and nodded in satisfaction. Steele quickly stowed his clearance card. As he rose, he once again fished his hunter pendant from inside his shirt and held it up inspection. The soldiers each side-stepped, barely allowing him a foot and a half of space to pass through. Once he was clear, they quickly closed ranks. He reached the guard station and was forced to go through the same identification process before the doors were unlocked and he was allowed to pass.

"What is going on here?" Steele asked the question to no one in particular. He spoke loud enough for all the soldiers to hear.

"Didn't you hear?" a young soldier volunteered.

Jackpot, Steele thought. He did his best to keep his face steady. There's always one or two chatters in the bunch. He turned slowly to face the boy. He wore the Templar uniform, but he didn't have any armor or weapons. He must be an apprentice, Steele guessed. The boy was carrying a stack of empty food trays. The top tray was loaded down with dirty cutlery and stacks of empty plates, bowls and cups. Steele quickly counted the trays. There should have been one for each hunter's prisoner, but the stack was two short.

He figured that they wouldn't risk feeding the sorceress he'd brought in. Since they'd put her hands behind her back for extra security, he was sure no one wanted to risk removing the magic restricting handcuffs. Besides, treating criminals like animals was one of the Templars' many unspoken perks. But which of the other hunters' prisoners didn't have a tray?

The boy lowered his voice and looked around nervously. Gossiping was fine as long as your direct superior didn't catch you in the act. Satisfied his commanding officer wasn't lurking behind any corners, he continued. "The information peddler brought in a subject."

"Really?"

"Yeah. A real viscious son of a vorak. He's tough too. Even with weighted hand cuffs and leg irons, he's giving the elite guard cause to think twice before they approach him."

"You don't say."

"Uh huh." The boy looked around again and then gestured with his head for Steele to come closer. He had to bend down in order for his ear to be level the with boy's mouth. "Word in the under region has it that your little sorceress and Whisp's capture worked closely together."

"How close are we talking?"

The boy shrugged. "Officially, I don't know anything. But unofficially—"

"What are you doing?" a higher ranking soldier snapped.

"N-n-nothing," the boy stammered.

"Exactly. And we don't keep you around just so you can waste the day standing around gossiping with the hunters."

"No sir. I mean, ma'am."

"Just get back to work. You've still got to feed the prisoners on the lower levels."

"Right away."

"Relax." Her tone softened. "Don't rush. A few hours without food might teach them a thing or two about obeying the law."

"Yes ma'am." The boy readjusted the stack of trays and scampered out of sight. "As for you," she said, turning her attention on Steele. "Visiting hours are officially over."

"I wasn't visiting. I was on my way to the hostelry and I must have made a wrong turn somewhere."

"Well, the prison transporter area has been restricted to official prisoner related travel only."

"Since when?"

"That's none of your business. Now, if you're here to check in on your capture, I'll give you five minutes. Otherwise get lost."

"I'm sure my capture is fine for today. Uh, if I may ask, when exactly are visiting hours?"

"0930 to 1330, 1800 to 2300 and 3250 to 3600 hours. Exceptions can be made if there's a medical issue, but in the case of your little sorceress I doubt that'll be necessary."

"Why do you say that?"

"It seems the doctor has been taking very good care of her. Stella?" the officer addressed one of the female guards.

"Ma'am"

"Why don't you show our guest from Realms Honor Guild the door?"

"Yes ma'am."

"No need." Steele raised his hands in a sign of defeat. "I know the way." He had no choice but to go back the way he came.

CHAPTER 9

Daphne groaned. She was accustomed to tossing and turning in her sleep, but sleeping propped against the wall made her neck stiff and the pain kept waking her up. She yawned. She wished she could stretch and rub the sleep from her eyes. The muscles in her shoulders and back were past aching. She was losing feeling in her arms. Daphne wiggled her fingers to help circulate her blood. Her arms tingled with the feeling of thousands of tiny needles traveling through her veins.

She slowly circled her neck and winced. During his last visit, Dr. Ouji had helped her find a good place on the wall to lean her head when she slept. It helped minimize the pain, but she still woke up with a crick in her neck. Through the translucent force field she could see that an increased number of soldiers had gathered. She let out a snort. *They must be beefing up my security,* she thought. *They're probably terrified I'll try to escape.*

"If only I really could get out of this mess," she complained.

Despite the force field blocking her view, she could make out more than just the guards' shadowy outlines. Her bruised eye was almost healed, but she'd lost her contacts the day she'd been brought on board. She should have had to squint and strain to make out any details, but over the past few days her vision seemed to be improving. She suspected it had something to do with Dr. Ouji's frequent visits.

She jumped, startled by the force field suddenly shutting off. She breathed a sigh of relief.

"Dr. Ouji. It's just you."

"Good evening subject 17A." He winked at Daphne. She couldn't help but smile. The stiff greeting was for the benefit of the guards on either side of the door.

Before the force field flashed back on, Daphne caught a glimpse of a new prisoner being brought in. She felt her eyes widen as a burly man and more than 15 Templar soldiers appeared out of nowhere. Even with handcuffs and leg irons shackled to each other to restrict his movements, he still managed to give them a run for their money. Good for him, Daphne thought. Even if he is guilty, they deserve to get some of their own medicine.

The force field flickered on again. This time, the energy wall was an opaque wall. The color reminded her of black pearls. It rippled with bits of blue and gray as though it were living marble. The doctor smiled in an effort to ease the growing worry showing on her face.

"Relax. It's standard procedure to do a complete physical the day before trial."

"Oh."

"Don't worry. They can't hear us either. A shield of this level blocks most sound."

"Okay."

"Is something wrong? You seem nervous."

"No. I'm fine."

The doctor followed Daphne's gaze with his own. Her eyes were locked on the holster at his waist. He should have known she would be put off by the gun. After all, he'd made a point of proclaiming his distaste for weapons to anyone who'd listen.

"Oh this. Don't worry. I'm not your executioner." He took the gun and placed it out of reach on the floor.

"Then why do you have a gun? I thought you didn't like weapons."

"It's a new order from the top. A temporary safety measure. We picked up a hunter whose brought a particularly dangerous criminal on board."

"That big guy from earlier?"

"Yes. He's a powerful sorcerer known for using illegal magic. He will use anyone within reach as a shield. Doctors are no exception. The commander sent out a direct order that everyone is to be armed at all times."

"Is it loaded?"

"The power cell is fully charged, if that's what you mean, but I'm not a quick draw."

"Well, then don't get too close to him. You're probably the only decent person onboard this ship. It'd be a shame if anything happened to you."

"Thank you for your kind words."

"I mean that. I'd probably have starved to death or died of abuse before now if it wasn't for you. I owe you one."

"Let's hope you never have to repay the debt."

"If it means getting out of prison alive, I'd gladly pay you back."

He smiled. "Here, I brought you something." He knelt down and opened the bag.

"What's all this?"

"Come now, we both know the guards aren't feeding you. The only food you've had since you've been here is the cold meat and water I sneak you."

The worry lines on her face melted away. He shifted the bag closer so she didn't have to crane her neck to see inside. Instead of his usual array of tools and salves, the box contained a miniature buffet. He undid the handcuffs and fixed her a plate of meat and gravy over lilac colored rice.

"You're not afraid I'll zap you with my magic and try to run away?" Daphne joked.

"You're about as harmless as a butterfly. On second thought, I take that back. It's an insult to the butterfly."

As he spooned food onto a plate, she circled her wrists, wiggled her fingers and flexed her arms. He watched her wince and listened to her joints creaked.

"Here, let me." He set the plate on the floor and took one of her arms in his. He gently massaged her skin to ease the painful tingling.

"Thanks." He shrugged and worked quickly on the other hand. "How does that feel?"

"Wow. The pain's gone. It's like magic….You weren't using magic were you?"

"No. You could say I've had a lot of practice."

"Thanks." Daphne picked up a spoon and set the plate in her lap. "This looks really good. What is it?"

"Endzian rice with a poultry sauce."

"Hmm."

"Hmm? Hmm what?"

"Nothing. It's just…where I come from, rice is white."

"How interesting."

"Don't tell me this is my last meal." Daphne paused with the spoon inches from her mouth.

"Last meal?"

"Well, you see, where I come from we do this thing where all the prisoners on death row—"

"I'm sorry…death row?"

"Death row is where they keep all the criminals who are supposed to get executed. The night before their execution, they get what's called a last meal."

"Why?"

"A humane courtesy."

"Oh. I see. Well, we don't have anything like that here I'm afraid."

"What: death row or a last meal?"

"The last meal. And even if we did have such a tradition, I doubt it's something you'll ever have to worry about."

"Really? You mean they're going to let me go?" she asked around a mouthful of food.

"I wouldn't be too hopeful of that. The Sages aren't known for their generosity. But, chances are execution won't be an issue. They'll probably just leave you locked up for the rest of your life."

"Starving to death in a cell with a once a day beating? I suppose it's better than nothing."

The doctor laughed. "You certainly have a dark sense of humor."

"Chalk it up to the five star Templar treatment. I'm recommending it to all my friends." Ouji smiled politely as Daphne laughed at her own joke.

"This chicken stuff is really good by the way."

"Chicken?"

"It's a type of poultry on Earth. Poultry just means bird."

"Ah, I see. Well thank you. It's my grandmother's recipe. I always make my own meals."

"Really? Why? Doesn't the ship have a kitchen?"

"It does, if you could call it that."

"I'm sure it's not that bad."

"Have you ever eaten ship food?" Daphne shook her head no. "Well, then you shouldn't judge."

"Fair enough." She took a few more bites as he poured two cups of an orange liquid. "What's that?"

"Citrus juice." Daphne took a sip and made a face. "Is something wrong?"

"Ugh. It tastes like bitter strawberries."

"Most juices here are fermented. It helps it keep."

"No wonder the soldiers are so mean. They must have permanent hangovers."

"The proof is very low, but I can mix in a little sugar if you like."

"Not to be picky, but I'd prefer water."

"So would I, but between the two of us, I've already used my drinking water ration for the next two weeks."

"Sorry about that."

He shrugged.

"Well beggars can't be choosers. I guess I'll have a little sugar then." As the sugar crystals dissolved, Daphne continued talking with her mouth full. "I know it's rude to talk while you eat, but I don't have a lot of time. Do you mind if I ask you a couple of questions?"

"Not at all."

"How did you get into this line of work? You know, caring for prisoners and such?"

"Well, it's kind of a family tradition. My ancestors actually started the Healers Guild. I can trace my lineage almost to the beginning of recorded history."

"Wow. That's…wow."

"Try not to be too impressed."

"But it's really amazing. I mean most people I know can barely trace their family back past one grandparent on either side. You're really lucky."

"I suppose. I get to do what I enjoy and help people, regardless of the politics. Some are stuck choosing a guild because they need a place to live or because they're trying to get rich."

"Really? In a world as advanced as this? Huh. I guess people are greedy no matter what dimension you're from."

"It's the goal of most Templar soldiers to earn a little glory, a little gold and a chance to move up the social ladder." Daphne scraped the last bit of sauce off the plate and handed it back to the doctor. "There's more if you want it."

"Please."

He doubled the portion and handed it back to her. She savored the feeling of the warm, thick sauce in her mouth. Daphne licked the plate after her second helping. She could hear her mother's voice in the back of her mind chastising her for eating as if she was starved. It wasn't like she hadn't had anything. Ouji had managed to sneak her some food over the past few days, but not enough to keep her satisfied. She handed the plate back to the doctor who packed it away. She wiped her face on a napkin and finished off the juice in her cup. There was a loud noise outside the door.

"What was that?"

"I don't know." Ouji pulled a small, round metal disk from his pocket and looked at it. His eyes darted back and forth quickly. Daphne craned her neck to see, but only caught a quick glimpse of a cape. "Quickly, put your hands behind your back."

Daphne did as she was told as Ouji hastily fastened the handcuffs. He shoved the remnants of her dinner inside his medical bag and closed it just as the force field flashed off. Four Templar soldiers stood in the door way. They looked over them suspiciously.

"Is everything alright in here doctor?" one of them asked. Probably the leader, the doctor thought.

"Fine. Can't you see I'm in the middle of an examination?"

"I'll bet he was feeding her like a pet," one of the others snapped. "You know he has a soft spot for the portal jumpers."

"I'm almost done here." He produced a small metal device that looked like a pen from inside his sleeve and waved it in front of her eyes.

"What's that for?" Daphne asked.

"Why don't you shut up and let the good doctor do his job?" the soldier barked.

"It's just a simple brain scan." Ouji said, taking on a professionally neutral attitude.

"Hurry up doctor," another of the soldiers slurred. "We want a word with the prisoner."

"You're off duty Martas and visiting hours are over. Now go away."

"You don't have the authority to order me." Martas argued, staggering forward.

"I do. But if you're not willing to listen, perhaps I should call the Sage's representative." Martas stopped advancing and took several unstable steps backward.

"Come on," he said to the others.

After they were gone, Ouji waited about 10 minutes before he checked the hall to make sure they wouldn't be coming back. He holstered his gun and picked up his bag, draping the strap diagonally over his shoulders.

"Wait."

"Yes Daphne?"

"I wanted to ask you about my eyes."

"I thought you might be curious. The type of lenses you were wearing were terribly archaic. You would never be able to replace them here, so I took the liberty of correcting your vision. I hope you don't mind."

"Thanks, but you didn't have to do that. I've been wearing glasses since the fourth grade."

"It also has to do with one of my guild's policies and fortunately the Sages adopted it as law. All prisoners have to be in perfect health in order to stand trial. Anything medical technology can correct must be fixed. That includes vision, limbs and so on."

"Well thanks." He nodded. "Good night doctor."

"Good night Daphne." He left and the force field flicked on instantly behind him. Once again she was alone in her metal box locked behind a translucent wall of energy.

CHAPTER 10

The amount of smoke kept the place dim. The air in the bar was bogged down with a rainbow haze of dark colors. Steele sat perched on the edge of a barstool. He had one foot planted on the floor and the other balanced against one of the chair's legs. He kept one hand beneath the counter where he could easily reach his laser knives. The other hand was in plain sight. He kept a loose grip on his drink. He did his best to block out the smoke by breathing through a folded scarf he'd pulled across his nose. He sipped slowly on a glass of thick apple beer. A thin layer of white foam floated on the top of the caramel colored liquid. He was on his fourth glass and was beginning to hear a humming sound inside his head.

He flashed a blue plastic-like card to catch the bartender's attention. She returned a brief nod to let him know she'd seen him, but she took her time heading in his direction. She finished polishing and stacking the warm glasses the kitchen boy had brought her. She topped off the drinks for a group of rowdy Templar soldiers. She didn't tilt the glass, so they ended up paying full price for a glass of mostly foam. The girl polished some spilled alcohol from the counter top, and finally sauntered over.

"What can I do for you hunter?" Her voice didn't carry with it any of the usual derision he was accustomed to from Templar members.

"The bill please."

"Paying up already? You hunters sure are light weights."

"I like to keep a level head when I travel."

"In other words, the other Templar are giving you a rough time. Don't let it bother you. They ride everybody hard. Most of them are embarrassed that guilds like yours are even necessary."

"I only do what I'm paid to do. They shouldn't take offense to that."

"Did you hear that fellas? He says we shouldn't take offense to being spied on." One drunk soldier shouted. His only response was a half-hearted cheer from a few nearby inebriated soldiers. The man roughly bumped into Steele's shoulder and leaned against the bar. He put his empty glass beside Steele's half full one. Gesturing with two fingers he addressed the bartender. "Fill 'er up missy."

"I'll get your check," she said to Steele.

"I don't get paid to spy," Steele answered calmly.

"Don't play stupid with me hunter. We all know your kind are just glorified watch dogs. Spying on the Templar and ratting us out to the mighty Sages." He spat on the floor.

"You should watch your tongue."

"Oh ho. Now he's telling me what to do."

"I'm just reminding you to watch your mouth. The Sages' representative is on board."

"And how's she gonna know what I said unless you tell her, spy?"

"I already told you, I don't get paid to spy."

Steele wasn't lying, but he wasn't telling the whole truth. Most hunter charters had guidelines for spying on the citizenry, but unless a contract specifically covered handling intelligence, the rules tended to go ignored. Unfortunately, the knowledge that spying on the people was part of the job description had created animosity between hunters and the people. This was especially true of the Templar who hated being watched as if they were always on the verge of planning a coup.

"Who cares if we knock around a prisoner or two right? They deserve what they get don't they? They need to be taught a lesson. Why else would they be here? Hmmn?"

The bartender returned with a full glass of a sedona colored liquid and a crystal tablet. Inside the translucent object was a circuit board and a complex arrangement of ultra-fine wires. Steele laid his blue card on the tablet and completed the transaction with his right thumbprint. He got up to leave, but the soldier barred him.

"I asked you a question."

"And I'm not obligated to answer."

"Leave him alone Martas," the bartender barked. "I already cleaned the bar twice this week. For once, I'd like to get through my shift without having to mop up someone's blood. Besides, you wouldn't want to disgrace the vows we took would you?"

"I don't remember any vows."

"Sure you do. You know, we fight for honor, justice and to protect the public good and all that."

"That's all a load of—"

"Nevertheless, it's the oath we swear."

Grumbling, he picked up his glass and tossed an amethyst encrusted merc on the counter. He slid his glass off the table, spilling some of his drink on the floor. Before vanishing into the haze, he wrapped an arm loosely around Steele's shoulders and leaned in close.

"Keep your hands off my sister or you'll find yourself in real trouble."

The bartender whipped a towel from beneath the counter. She swatted Martas' arm and returned the towel to its hiding place in one smooth motion. The towel was a blur as it cracked past Steele's ear.

"Get on. And stop harassing the customers. I'm a big girl. I wouldn't be worth my cape and sword if I couldn't handle one bounty hunter."

Still grumbling Martas pushed his way through the crowd and disappeared from view. Steele tossed back his cup and finished off his glass. He rose to his feet. The bartender grabbed his wrist and pulled him close. Her physical strength was impressive. With her delicate looking frame, he would never have suspected she was capable of pulling him off balance. Her eyes darted around nervously.

"Listen, if I were you, I'd tell that doctor friend to watch his back. Some of the soldiers don't like how friendly he is with the prisoners. Especially that devil witch you brought in."

"I wouldn't worry about it. He may not look like much, but he's quite the accomplished mage."

"Maybe, but all the same…Don't say I didn't warn you."

"I'll tell him."

She let him go and pretended to look busy polishing the counter. She pocketed the golden, amethyst dusted coin.

"Oh, and you didn't hear this from me, but he's wasting his time anyway, making friends with that one."

"Oh?"

"Portal Sickness my foot. She may have the doctor fooled, but thank the cosmos the Sages have some sense."

"They've already made a ruling? But the prisoner hasn't even been to trial."

"What do you live under a rock? Those things are all show. All the verdicts are decided without ever hearing a shred of evidence."

"Isn't that illegal?"

"People don't care about that as long as they feel like they saw justice done. All you need is a little money in the right pocket. Me personally, I hope they put her in the shock chamber."

"My money's on the firing squad," the kitchen boy chimed in as he brought in a fresh supply of clean glasses.

"No way," an off duty squadron leader added in his two cents worth as he placed his cup on the counter for a refill. "I say it's the grater."

Despite his nose guard, Steele choked on the smoke from the man's cigarette. He gave the bartender a casual two-finger salute good-bye and slipped into the corridor. The clear force field over the door was warm against his skin. The mild shield acted as a biological filter. It kept the smoke from seeping into the ship's main air system. After last call, the room would be depressurized so the smoke could be exchanged with fresh air from outside. It was designed to save energy by reducing the stress on the ship's air filtering and recycling system. Unfortunately, it didn't do anything to clean the smell out of his clothes.

Steele striped off his scarf and shook out the wrinkles. A few ashes trapped in the folds of the fabric scattered to the floor. He flipped his clearance card between his knuckles as he walked toward the nearest transporter. Whisp's capture had managed to break free five times since he'd been brought on board. The last time he'd escaped, he'd managed to make it to the escape pods. The soldiers barely caught him before he launched. Unfortunately for the rest of the ship, each failed attempt resulted in heightened security measures. Every extra check point was just another hassle, and forced Steele to spend more time in contact with the Templar—something he could definitely do without.

"Sorry Ouji," he muttered as his shoulder grazed against the doctor's.

"Don't worry about it. I'm sure it was my fault." Ouji replied absent mindedly. The doctor paused and looked up from the file he was reading. "Steele?"

"Lost in research as always?"

"You could say that. I was just on my way back from doing the prison rounds." He adjusted the strap of the bag on his shoulder.

"It's been a while. We should make time to catch up," Steele offered.

"I've got some time if you want to join me for tea."

Steele tried not to cringe outwardly. He wasn't in the mood for conversation. He was only trying to be polite. But it was hard to deny his old friend, especially when he was in such an obviously good mood.

"Sure."

"Excellent. My office is this way."

CHAPTER 11

Steele followed closely behind Dr. Ouji. The doctor passed through every check point without having to show his credentials. The soldiers all snapped to attention, saluted, and then stepped aside. They gave the doctor and his guest more than enough room to pass through the center of the hall, waiting until he was clear before closing ranks. The respect they afforded him was significantly different from the lack of respect they showed Steele and the other bounty hunters.

Steele followed on the doctor's heels at the security station, but did his best to hang back in between check points. He had known Ouji long enough to know how much he hated the smell of alcohol and smoke.

"You reek," Ouji snapped. The comment didn't carry much of a sting. He'd never been able to hide when he was happy.

"I know. Sorry. I know you hate it, but hunters aren't allowed to eat in their rooms."

The metal doors to the doctor's office slid open. Ouji practically danced over the threshold. He wheeled quickly and pushed Steele back.

"You wait here." Ouji stepped back and pushed a button on a nearby wall panel. Warm light descended on Steele. It slowly swept up and down his frame five times before shutting off. Ouji waved him in and the doors whooshed closed behind him.

"Is it just me, or are you in a good mood today?"

The doctor didn't answer. His attention was focused on the tea preparations. He carefully ladled water from a metal canister into a glass ball balanced carefully over a Bunsen burner. Steele shuffled his feet as the doctor lit a flame to heat the cloudy water.

"No offense Ouji, but the water quality standards for doctors has really gone to the dogs."

Ouji chuckled softly and shook his head. "The water's not as bad as all that. This is from the recycled water systems."

"Don't tell me they've got you drinking shower water."

"It's only for a little while. I must've forgotten to keep track of my ration."

"Feeding the prisoners again?" The doctor stared intently at the water as it flowed through a series of glass tubes. "Relax. You know I don't get paid to spy."

"Maybe, but your psychic magic defense is less than basic, if that. Rumor has it that you're sharing a room with him."

"If by him you mean the Whisperer, then they're right." Steele folded his arms across his chest and leaned against the wall. "You could always borrow a little water from the medical surplus."

"That water is for emergencies."

"When was the last time there was an actual emergency?"

"I'd risk getting fired."

"Please, commander Hyric would be thrilled to see you come over to his side. If nothing else, you'd fit in a little better with the soldiers."

"The path to corruption is a slippery slope. It may start with a little water, but who knows where it would lead?"

The clear water flowed through coiled glass tubes and poured into a ceramic pot. Ouji pulled two chipped ceramic mugs from a drawer beneath his desk and set them on the table. He poured an equal amount of water in each cup. He then added three scoops of green powder. The water frothed and a thick layer of green foam rose to the top.

"I hate the instant stuff, but the ship store doesn't stock anything decent." He sat down at a small round table in the corner and gestured for Steele to have a seat. "Now the Endzians, they know what true quality is."

Steele shrugged as he took a seat. "Can't say I know the difference. You can't afford anything decent on a hunter salary."

"You could if you took higher paying cases."

"The higher paying cases are risky."

"I thought hunters didn't choose their profession for its job security or health plan. There's real money to be made in cases like Daphne's."

"And portal jump my way into an early grave? I think not." Steele took a sip of the tea and made a face. "The flavor seems off."

Ouji took a sip and frowned. "The dirty cheat. He cut it with blossom powder."

"Ask for a refund."

"I can't. All sales final."

"It's not like you to get caught in such an obvious trap."

"I've been distracted lately."

"By my newest capture no doubt." The doctor shrugged. "How is the little sorceress?" Steele asked.

"Fit enough for trial. Not that you or anyone else really cares." His frowned deepened as he watched Steele shrug. "You're not the least bit concerned that this girl could be innocent? I've lost count of the number of portal cases that ended in double executions. First the innocent double from some other reality and then two or three years down the line when they finally catch the real criminal. Sometimes they just let the second capture go free, when he's the one who's actually guilty."

"The system may have a few flaws, but don't allow those doe eyes to fool you. That girl is guilty."

"Like Jonnie was guilty?"

"Jonnie was guilty and he paid for his crimes!"

"Just because no one else was brought in doesn't mean you were right. You obviously didn't think so, or you wouldn't avoid portal jump cases like toxin. Admit it. You were put off by the Sages' lack of concern for the temporal inconsistency."

"Portae Languorem was just something pantywaists like you invented so they could avoid making any real decisions."

"The punishment should fit the crime. And before we authorize an execution, we should be certain we have the right person in custody. People are not disposable!"

The office door swooshed open. "Is everything okay doctor?" Ouji's assistant asked. Like Ouji, she wore a medical version of the Templar uniform. The shoulders of her cape had brass apprentice symbols pinned on them.

She took a nervous step back as she surveyed the scene. The two men stared at each other. Ouji's hands were trembling. He was halfway out of his chair. Steele locked his jaw to keep his face muscles steady. He'd forgotten how fast Ouji could move. If it hadn't been for the assistant's interruption, they would certainly have crossed a line in their friendship.

"Yes, everything's fine." Ouji's voice was calm and steady as he settled back into his seat. "We were just discussing politics. Do you need something Angela?"

"I just thought you'd like to see a copy of the official medical report." She held out a blue memory chip.

"Thank you. Uh, which prisoner is this for?"

"The young sorceress sir." She set the chip on the table and bowed respectfully before leaving.

As soon as she was gone, Ouji rose from the table and walked to his desk. He carefully pushed aside Daphne's confiscated items and slipped the chip into the desktop projector. From where he sat, Steele could see the tips of Ouji's ears turning red.

"I don't believe this."

"What?"

"Why don't you see for yourself our justice system at work?"

Steele stepped close enough to read the screen. His mouth dropped open. Everything in the report had been forged, including Dr. Ouji's signature. He watched the doctor's shoulders drop. Ouji let out a defeated sigh and sank into his office chair.

"Damn."

"Is this sort of thing typical?" Steele didn't know what else to say. He'd never seen his friend look so defeated.

"I supposed I should be used to it. Things like this happen all the time. Ever since the government started paying bonuses for every convicted criminal that's brought in. Rather than put any effort into catching and punishing the real criminals, commanders like Hyric just turn in false reports. Everyone involved gets a percentage in exchange for keeping their mouth shut."

"What about the appeals process?"

"I've tried sticking my neck out for the ones I really believe in. The Sages are no different from the Templar. The oaths they take are empty. They're people whose souls can all be bought. Since I took the position as head medical officer on this ship, I've probably seen one of every 30 portal cases go free."

"Then why invest yourself so much in the welfare of one prisoner?"

"If not me than who? Innocent or guilty, I do what I do because I believe everyone deserves a little humanity in their final hours."

"What's that thing?"

"Huh?" Ouji looked down. Daphne's confiscated belongings stared back at him. Without realizing it, he'd been fingering the cross necklace. "I don't know. It belongs to Daphne. It's got some gold in it and a couple of cheap crystals, but it doesn't seem very valuable. The symbol must have some sort of significance. It really is a shame. I was looking forward to returning it to her."

"Ouji—"

"Steele, you know, I forgot I have some work I need to finish. Maybe you and I can catch up some other time?"

"Yes. Of course."

Steele listened to the metal doors swoosh close. There was a faint computerized beep as the doctor locked the door behind him.

CHAPTER 12

Daphne's fingers moved swiftly over the piano keys. The piano had been recently tuned, so the sound was perfect. Her mother had dusted the piano about an hour ago so the wood still smelled of lemon Pledge. She hummed to herself as she played in time with the metronome. The clicking of the device's pendulum was giving her a headache. Playing in time with the rhythmic tapping was harder than her teacher had made it look. No matter how many times she practiced, she always seemed to fall behind. She glanced at the egg timer her mother had put on top of the television. Only 15 more minutes before I can take a break, she reminded herself.

"It's too hot for this," she groaned. She was sweating and her glasses had slid to the tip of her nose. The breeze from the oscillating fan turned the page in her music book to another song. The book was only there for security. She really didn't need it. She had the song memorized.

"Stop looking at your hands," Addison chided.

The sudden sound of her mother's voice startled her and Daphne botched the last few bars. Her mother laughed.

"Mom, seriously, you know I hate it when you do that."

"Your teacher's just going to get on your case again about memorizing." Her mother said, standing in front of the fan, her dark auburn curls bouncing in the breeze. "You know she wants you to read the music."

"Addie, stop blocking the air," her father groaned from the couch.

"I can't help it if I memorized it. I've played it like a hundred thousand times."

"Still—"

"Leave her alone," her father sighed. "Who cares about fingering as long as she can play it?"

"Exactly." Daphne agreed.

"Because Emory," her mother argued, "it's not about just playing it. She's supposed to learn proper technique."

"Daphne, aren't you ready for a break?" he asked, his voice still holding on to traces of his Irish accent. Addison giggled and shook her head. Even after 18 years of marriage, she still couldn't wrap her brain around the irony of an Irish man with chocolate skin.

"Yes." Daphne slid eagerly off the piano bench as Emory forced the timer back to zero. Addison rolled her eyes.

"You two just want to watch T.V."

"She's been practicing that song for days. I think it's perfect."

"I agree with daddy."

"You would. Fine one hour and then—" A bright light flashed above her.

"Did you see that?" Daphne asked.

The words seemed more in her head than out loud. The room spun and she was suddenly looking up at a gaping hole in the ceiling. She looked around in panic to find everything had changed. The couch and piano were gone. Her parents were crouched on the floor near her. She reached out to them, but they seemed to slide away from her. The more she reached for them, the further away they seemed to get. It was as if she was running but her body wasn't moving.

Daphne looked up and stared at a cloudy gray sky as dust and debris rained down on her. She threw up her arms to protect herself and screamed, but no sound came out. She could feel a hand on her throat. She struggled to get away, but something was holding her down. She flailed and struggled as she felt her stomach lurch as her body rose into the air.

"Daphne, Daphne. Wake up."

Panting frantically, she forced her eyes open. Her vision was blurry and her head felt wrapped in fuzz. As her breathing slowed, she felt whatever was on her mouth move. She blinked as her eyes adjusted to the darkness in the room. As a face came into focus, she completely relaxed and allowed herself to be put in a sitting position.

"Dr. Ouji, what are you doing?"

"Shh." He put his fingers to his lips and whispered. "Daphne, are you alright? The guards called me. They said you were screaming."

"Was I? I think I was dreaming."

"Having a nightmare it seems."

"No, not really. It's strange. I've tried so hard to see them when I close my eyes, to remember the way they laugh, but I couldn't. And just now they were clear as day."

"Who?"

"My mom and my dad, I could hear their voices. I could see their faces." The doctor nodded quietly. "Dr., I'm sorry they called you down here or nothing."

"It's not a total waste, since I'm here, I may as well stay a while."

"Won't you get in trouble? Aren't visiting hours are over?"

"They are, but I have something for you."

He held out his hand. Resting in his palm was the cross necklace. Daphne gasped, a smile spreading across her face. For a brief moment her fear and weariness melted away. She wished she could reach out and touch it.

"How did you find it? I never thought I'd get any of my things back." The doctor fastened it around her neck and she watched it vanish. She could still feel the metal against her skin.

"I put a spell on it. This way you can keep it with you."

"Thank you, but why?"

"I don't know what this is for, but I just had a feeling that I should give it back to you."

"Ouji?" He smiled, but even in the dark Daphne could tell there was a different light in his eyes. "Go back to sleep, I'm sorry I bothered you."

Ouji slipped quietly into the hall. He spoke to the guards before leaving. Daphne lay back down and felt the cross slide up the chain. She tossed her head and wiggled her shoulders until the edge of the metal touched her cheek. It was comforting to have it back. Even though it no longer smelled like the perfume she was wearing the day she'd been kidnapped, if she closed her eyes, she could almost feel her mother's hands pushing her hair back as she fastened the clasp. As she felt herself drifting back to sleep, she smiled.

"Hey you."

Daphne moaned and rolled onto her stomach. She turned her head toward the wall and murmured.

"I said get up," the soldier snapped, yanking her to her feet.

"What?"

"Come on. You don't want to be late for court."

Daphne's stomach quickly began to twist into knots. She felt dizzy as all the blood rushed from her head. Court? Dr. Ouji had given her reason to hope that she might actually get out of this mess. It's too bad they don't have public defenders, she thought. If they did, I would have an even better shot at this. The lights in the hall seemed brighter to her than she remembered.

The Templar soldiers led her to the end of the hall. They surrounded her on a slightly raised patch of metal. The hallway faded away in a flash of bright light. When her eyes stopped seeing spots, she took in her surroundings. The walls had changed from metal to stone and there were large windows every few feet. Her sneakers squeaked against the freshly waxed floor. The soldiers' boots thudded solidly against the stone floor.

Their footsteps echoed in the empty hall. Daphne shivered. She could hear her heart pounding in her ears. Her knees shook with every step. She counted her steps and took slow, measured breaths. "Don't panic, don't panic, don't panic," was all she could think to tell herself. The soldiers stopped before a heavy wooden door. The leader knocked on the door and it swung open.

"There's no one in here." Her voice echoed in the almost empty room. There was a chair by the door and small, curtained off alcove in the corner. They pushed her until her feet crossed the threshold. The room was bathed in what appeared to be sunlight, but there were no windows. The walls were a bright white and the floor tiles had a simple blue flower painted in the center of each tile.

"Take a shower and change your clothes." The door slammed and she heard the lock click.

"How am I supposed to take a bath with my hands tied behind my back?" As if in response to her question, the shower switched on. The water rushed out and steam began to fill the air. The handcuffs clattered to the floor. Daphne stood rooted to one spot. This is really creepy, she thought. She couldn't shake the feeling that this situation would fit right into a horror movie. Daphne turned quickly and tried the door. It was locked.

"You only have an hour. Either bathe or show up to court filthy." The voice came from a speaker hidden somewhere in the ceiling.

"I guess I don't have a choice," she muttered. Daphne stared at the thin yellow shower curtain. As she approached it her mind went back to all the Holocaust movies they'd watched in history last year. As she stripped off her sweater and jeans she prayed, "Please God let this be a shower and not a gas chamber."

She held her breath and eased her fingertips into the stream of water. She breathed a sigh of relief to find it was warm and soapy. It was the perfect temperature. It was hot, but not scalding. She stepped into the shower. She closed her eyes while soapy water rained on her. As she washed her hair and rubbed her skin, the soft floral scent of the soap reminded her that she hadn't bathed in days. How did the doctor stand it? She wondered. She squeezed her eyes closed until the floral scent faded and the water began to run clear.

She stepped out as the water shut off. The shower vanished. Hovering in its place was a plain white dress. It looked like a Victorian style night gown. Daphne looked around for her clothes, but they were gone. This is crazy, she thought.

"You can't expect me to wear that," she said, her voice echoing off the walls. "It's practically see through."

The temperature of the tile floor began to rise. At first the heat was pleasant against the soles of her feet, but the temperature continued to increase rapidly. She bounced on the tip toes of one foot to the other until her skin felt as if it would blister.

"Alright, alright!" Daphne screamed. "You win."

She reached out frantically. The tips of her fingers touched the gown and the outfit magically appeared on her body. Her hands were once again cuffed behind her back. Her ankles were also shackled and the two sets of restraints were chained together. The temperature of the floor returned to normal and the wooden door swung open. The squadron of Templar soldiers waited for her to shuffle into the corridor.

"A warning would have been nice."

The soldiers said nothing. They turned her back toward the north end of the hallway. Her bare feet left wet footprints. Her wet hair was cold against her back. She stumbled due to the weight and unfamiliarity of the chains.

"This is really inhumane. I can barely move my feet. It's like trying to walk with your shoelaces tied together."

Still the soldiers said nothing. They walked her to another heavy wooden door. The door opened and the soldiers took up guard positions around it.

"Go!" the leader snapped.

Daphne hesitated. He drew his sword. The sound of metal being unsheathed froze the blood in her chest. Her heart skipped a beat, but the terror was enough to give her legs motivation.

Daphne took a deep breath and took two small steps forward. The door slammed shut behind her. Once again she heard the sound of a lock. The room had no windows. She stood in complete darkness for what seemed like hours before she was blinded by bright lights.

CHAPTER 13

The sudden brightness temporarily blinded her. Even though she couldn't see, Daphne's ears still worked. The roar of the crowd was so loud it blocked out the sound of her pounding heart. Slowly, her eyes adjusted to the light and she wished she could fade back into darkness. She was on a small platform hovering in the air above thousands of people. She was surrounded on all sides. The rotunda's seating continued to soar above her.

She staggered backward as vertigo gripped her. The sturdy railing encircling her kept her from falling. Daphne took a deep breath and looked up. She squinted as she tried to follow the direction of a support beam. She was certain the bright light above her wasn't the sun. It was bright enough, however, it didn't give off any warmth.

Before her hovered a judges' bench. Behind it sat a robed man and two robed women. They watched her with cold, accusing eyes. The first woman looked to be about 40. She looked down her nose at Daphne. Her robe was a deep sunset orange trimmed in black. The other woman was much older. Her hair was beginning to gray. Her robe was white and trimmed in black with a silver leaf design. The man sat in the center. His robe was dark green and was also trimmed in black. His hair was completely gray and his hairline was receding. He had a long beard which reached to his navel.

The man stood slowly and raised his arms in the air. The place grew deathly silent. He stared intently at Daphne. She wished she could make her heart stop beating so loudly. He lowered his arms and took his seat. When he spoke, his powerful voice reverberated through the space. Despite the depth of his voice, his icy tone gave her no cause to hope.

"Diamara Katz, you are aware of the charges against you."

Daphne stood frozen. Why are they still calling me that? She wondered. Didn't the doctor say I had a strong chance to go free?

"Speak!"

"Y-y-yes sir," she stammered.

"What say you in your defense?"

"That you're wrong."

"Pardon?"

She wanted to kick herself. I can't believe I just insulted the judge, she thought. Just keep talking, she shouted mentally. "Be respectful," she murmured to herself. She cleared her throat and addressed the man again. "I think there's been a mistake. My name isn't—"

"We're well aware of what you would have us believe," the woman in orange interrupted.

"But—"

"You will be silent!" the other woman screamed, rising to her feet. "You will speak only when you have been asked a direct question."

The sternness in the woman's voice frightened Daphne. She staggered backward and fell against the railing. Her platform wobbled. She screamed and quickly shut her mouth. In her haste, she bit her tongue. Daphne tried to steady her breathing as she struggled to her feet. She swallowed the saltiness of her blood.

"Considering the charges against you and the evidence presented to this court," the man continued, "we the Sages of the high court of Capytal, find you guilty." The assembly erupted in wild cheers. The man stood and raised his arms. "Silence!" His deep voice boomed out and a hush fell over the room. "We hereby sentence you to death by torture."

Again the assembly erupted into cheers. Daphne's knees gave way. She couldn't breathe. Her vision blurred and the room spun. The judge continued to talk and the crowd shouted in approval. For Daphne, the sounds were muffled as if her ears were immersed in water. The world felt removed from her, as though she were a ghost, seeing the events through a fog.

The courtroom faded away and the heavy wooden door swung open. The Templar soldiers lifted her crumpled figure off the floor. They half carried, half dragged her down the hall until she began to move her legs on her own.

"This isn't right," she wanted to scream, but the words that did escape were barely audible. "This can't be happening. You've got it wrong. Please, don't do this." She was aware her pleas were falling on deaf ears. With each step the hidden cross bounced against her collarbone. Her tears felt cold against her cheeks. Her shackle chains scraped against the floor. The sound seemed to come from a distance.

"Hail Mary, mother of God, pray for us sinners, now and at the hour of our death."

"Be quiet," the lead soldier snapped.

"For though I walk through the valley of the shadow of death, I will fear no evil, for thou art with me—"

"I said shut up."

She was aware she was mixing the prayers, but the more she struggled to remember, the more solid those words became. They took over her mind and she couldn't think past them to make sense of the jumble of words and images in her mind. She could see flashes of everything from her life except what she desperately wanted to see: her parents' faces. Even the details from last night's dream were beyond reach.

Daphne dragged her feet as she was led down flight after flight of spiraling stairs. Her bare skin seemed to stick to the floor tiles. Each level of the building had fewer and fewer windows until she found herself in what could only have been described as a dungeon. While clean, the place had the musty smell of a cellar. They guided her to a heavy metal door. The lead soldier handed her execution order to a young man dressed in white.

He read it carefully, signed it with his thumbprint and handed it back.

"What is that she's mumbling?" he asked.

The lead soldier shrugged. "She's been muttering since the verdict. Just ignore her."

The Templar soldiers held her still while the executioner carefully removed her restraints and secured her to a wall. One by one they filed into the hallway and watched as he sealed the heavy metal door. The soldiers turned to leave.

"Hold it. I need someone to stay and verify that the task was completed." There was silence. "If no one volunteers, I will be forced to pick one of you." he added.

"I'll stay," the lowest ranking officer grumbled.

The others breathed audible sighs of relief. Once they were gone, the executioner walked to a computer panel and swiped a white security card. A whistling sound came from the chamber, followed by a sound like thunder and lightning, then screaming. After a few moments, the screaming died away. The executioner's lips moved slowly as he counted to five. He then increased the voltage and swiped the card again. First came the whistling. It lasted longer this time as the machine charged and then the crackle, followed by Daphne's screams.

With each swipe of the card, the executioner flinched. He cringed at the sound of the machine charging and ground his teeth as he listened to the prisoner's screams. The soldier shuffled his feet and scrubbed at an imaginary stain with his toe as he resisted the urge to cover his ears. He didn't want to risk looking weak in front of someone younger than he was.

"If it bothers you that much, why don't you just change jobs?" the soldier asked.

"It's not the killing that bothers me," he answered calmly. "It's listening to them die that's the problem."

"Like I said, why not get a different job?"

"I can't. I'm not a graduate. I wouldn't be able to pay my apprentice debt."

"Why did you choose this job in the first place?"

"I didn't choose it." he paused, adjusted the setting on the machine and swiped the card again. "I was selected. My parents died when I was a boy. I had nowhere to go. The old man who runs this place said he'd take me in. I was young and afraid of starving. I would've agreed to anything."

He raised his hand to swipe the card again, but the soldier grabbed his wrist. "Wait. Do you hear that?"

"I don't hear anything."

"Exactly. I think she stopped screaming a while ago."

"Doesn't matter, she's still alive."

"How can you tell?"

He gestured to the computer monitor. "Her vital signs are still good. So far, I've kept the voltage pretty low."

"But she's unconscious."

He shrugged again.

"But how is it torture if she can't feel anything?"

"You wouldn't be trying to sneak in a more humane death?" the master asked, entering the room through a back door. He was accompanied by the bearded sage and an imposing man with thick black hair on his head and face.

"Humane isn't in our vocabulary," the executioner replied.

"Never mind," the master said casually. He pushed the younger man aside and proceeded to shut down the machine. "This prisoner's free to go."

"Sir?" the executioner asked. "I've never known an execution order to be rescinded."

"Well, there's a first time for everything. We've been ordered to release her and see that she's taken care of. Sages' orders."

CHAPTER 14

"I don't see why she has to be my responsibility," Steele raged. He slammed the palms of his hands on top of the Guild Master's desk. Hyron leaned back in his chair and cracked his knuckles before taking a long drag from his cigar. "Don't just sit there smoking yourself into a stupor. Say something."

"Alright. If you insist, I will say it. This entire mess is your fault. Need I remind you it was you who brought in the wrong subject?" Guild Master Hyron barked back.

"I haven't handled a portal jump case in years."

"Steele, I'm surprised. It isn't like you to make excuses."

"I'm not making excuses. I'm simply stating a fact. I told you I didn't want the job."

"My hands were tied. Since you were the one who captured her originally, the Templar felt you'd be the most capable hunter for the job. Of course, given the time since your last portal case, it's only natural to see how you could have made such an obvious mistake."

"I followed procedure! And this wouldn't have happened if I hadn't been ordered to take the case." Steele seethed

"Well if you could tell the difference between a 30 year old woman and a child, this discussion wouldn't be necessary," Cinnamon added.

"Shut up Cinnamon." Steele snapped. "Why are you even here?"

"I have business."

"Not right now you don't," Hyron added. "This doesn't concern you." Cinnamon shrugged and popped a small piece of fruit in his mouth. He settled into an armchair beside the door.

"I won't do it." Steele continued.

"You will." Hyron pressed.

"Why? Why do I have to be the one?"

"Because it's the law," Cinnamon chirped.

"I don't believe this." Steele groaned. "You expect me to play babysitter?"

"Either you take care of her or the guild has to, and I'm not in the business of cleaning up the members' messes."

"How did she manage it?" Cinnamon interjected.

"Manage what?" Steele asked.

"Sorry, I was just wondering aloud. It had to have been that spell the soldiers said she was whispering. I'll bet it was some sort of trick."

"The way I hear it," Hyron replied, "that doctor friend of yours finally learned how the game is played. A little money in the right pocket and she's out on the street."

"No. Surely you don't think Ouji bought her freedom."

"Sure seems that way doesn't it," Cinnamon laughed.

"And just what are the Sages planning on telling the people?"

Cinnamon let out a loud laugh. "This is where it gets good."

"Be quiet or get out!" Hyron ordered.

"It seems they're going to say you tampered with the evidence in order to get a conviction. They're going to be investigating all your old cases. Your perfect little reputation is tarnished."

"Cinnamon!" Hyron snapped.

"I've never handled a case dishonestly in my life."

"Relax Steele," Hyron said calmly. "It's all just a cover. They can't very well let someone like her out of prison without giving the people a good reason."

"It's not the inquiry that bothers me, on paper or otherwise. It's the girl."

"What's the matter?" Cinnamon asked, "Can't handle one magic-less little girl?"

"I don't like it."

"Like it or not, until the portal to her world reopens, she's your responsibility." Hyron finished.

Daphne was surrounded by white. Her body was floating on a mountain of something soft. In the air she could smell the faint citrus scent of yellow roses. Looking down at her was the smiling face of a woman with white blonde hair. The woman's hair was swept into a fishtail braid that was coming undone at the ends. The style looked as though it had been slept in. The hair closet to her scalp was puffy. Even slept in, the woman's hair framed her head perfectly. The light streaming between the pale strands created a glow as if she were surrounded by a halo.

I'm dead, Daphne thought. But if I was dead, would I still be able to think? She wiggled her fingers and winced. Even breathing caused her body to ache. Nope, not dead, she concluded. She tried wiggling her toes. They barely moved, weighed down by the down quilt on top of her. The woman's lips were like soft pink paint on porcelain. They moved slowly as she spoke. Daphne couldn't hear her. I haven't gone deaf, she reassured herself. She's speaking another language. I just don't understand her.

She could see something out of the corner of her eye. It took her a minute to realize it was the woman's fingers. Is she stroking my hair? The woman's lips moved again. This time Daphne could faintly hear sounds; however, she still couldn't make out the words. This really must be torture, she thought. They strap me down and electrocute me, and then they have someone fix me up just so they can do it again. Her heart was pounding. She struggled to sit up.

"Shhh." The woman whispered softly. She pressed gently against Daphne's shoulders and held her down. "Please don't struggle. I promise that you're safe here."

Daphne stopped struggling. "I, I can hear you," she croaked. "I mean, I can understand what you're saying. I'm not deaf."

The woman laughed and smiled as she brushed a curl off Daphne's forehead. "Get some rest Daphne. We can talk when you're well. I promise I'll explain everything later."

"Wait. How do you know my name?"

"Rest."

Daphne could feel her eyes closing. She wanted to stay awake. Fear gripped her as darkness encroached. She didn't want to wake up and find herself still chained to the dungeon wall. The woman's hands were warm and soft against the side of her face. Daphne's pounding heart slowed to a normal pace and she felt her body relax.

When she opened her eyes again, the woman was gone. The light streaming in from the window was a mixture of purples, blues and pinks. She lay still and let her eyes sweep the room. It was large enough for a twin sized bed and a few moderately sized pieces of furniture. On the wall was a flat computer screen. Daphne couldn't make any sense of the glowing symbols. Across from the window was a cherry stained door. The door was slightly ajar.

Resting on a tray table beside the bed was a platter of light foods. There was a bowl of soup, some crackers and a glass of water with fresh berries floating in it. Daphne gritted her teeth as she pushed back the edge of the feather comforter. It still hurt to move. She winced as she tried to bend her left arm in an effort to sit up. There was an IV protruding from the bend of her arm. Daphne grabbed the covers with her right hand and pulled herself up.

There was a quiet tap on the door. Before she could reply, the door was pushed open. A halo of white blonde hair came into view. It was quickly followed by a smiling face as the woman she assumed was her nurse poked her head inside the room. Her blue eyes sparkled like prisms in the twilight. She opened the door further and glided into the room.

"Oh good, you're awake," she breathed. She barely touched the edge of the computer screen and the lights in the room came on. The strips of light ran the entire length of the ceiling. "How's that?"

"It's still dark."

"Well, I don't want to make it too bright. You've been through a lot today. Are you hungry?"

"Who are you?"

"My name is Kember Roth."

"Where am I?"

"Healers Guild Hospital in the city of Capytal."

"Why are you helping me?"

"We can talk about that later. Are you hungry?"

"No." Her stomach growled. Daphne rolled her eyes. Her stupid stomach had to give her away.

"It's alright. I promise it's not poison."

"Then you won't mind tasting it first."

Kember laughed. "Dr. Ouji warned me you'd be suspicious." She pulled a chair close to the side of the bed and sat down. She balanced the tray on her lap and scooped a spoonful of soup into her mouth. Daphne watched her swallow before she was satisfied.

"The hospital's famous for its soup," Kember volunteered.

Daphne's hand trembled as she struggled to lift the spoon to her lips. Hot droplets of soup dripped onto her chin. The soup was almost too watery to be appetizing. The vegetables and noodles had been cooked so long they dissolved the moment they came in contact with her tongue. No salt or recognizable spices had been added to it either. Daphne sighed. The only decent food she'd had since coming here was the meager amounts of food and water Dr. Ouji had slipped her while she was on the Templar ship.

"Here, let me help you." Kember offered. She wiped Daphne's chin with a napkin. Her touch was extremely delicate. She took the spoon from Daphne's quivering hand and began to feed her. After five bites, Daphne couldn't take sitting up anymore. She leaned back against the pillows. The overstuffed cushions cradled her aching body. They reminded her of gigantic marshmallows.

"Is there something wrong with the food?"

"It's tasteless." She wheezed a few short breaths of fresh air into her lungs. "It hurts to breathe, swallow and basically everything."

"The shock chamber is probably one of the cruelest punishments there is. And I'm sure it doesn't help that this soup is bland."

"I thought you said the hospital was famous for it."

"That I did, but I suppose I should have told you why."

Daphne's head was spinning. Her eyes felt like they were rolling backward into her brain. Kember put the soup back on the tray and pulled the curtains closed. She tapped the edge of the computer screen and the lights shut off. She moved the tray table closer to the bed. She took the soup but left the crackers and the water.

"Good night Daphne," she spoke softly and closed the door quietly behind her.

"You son of a Vorak. What the frell do you think you're doing?" Steele roared.

"Making a sandwich, but I didn't know it was a crime," the doctor joked as Steele stormed into his office.

"Don't fool with me Ouji. I'm not stupid. I know it was you. Have you lost your mind?"

"What the frell has gotten into you?"

"You bought that sorceress out of her execution."

"What sorceress?"

"That girl from my portal jump case."

"You mean Daphne? Steele, my friend, you are sorely misinformed. First of all, that girl is no sorceress and secondly, I did no such thing."

"You did. You had to have done it. No one else bothers to get attached to the prisoners the way you do."

"You're insane. I filed an appeal as soon as the trial ended, nothing more."

"Really?"

"Yes really."

"What's the status?"

"In process."

"Why would you file an appeal on her behalf? You don't know her."

"And you do? Tell me Steele, what do you know about her?"

"I know she's guilty."

"Well, I think she's innocent."

"You say that about 90 percent of the inmates who pass through your office. You're naïve." The doctor shrugged.

"Maybe so, but if I know Kember, she was at the trial. What does she think?"

Steele mumbled.

"I'm sorry, I didn't quite catch that."

"She took one look at her and proclaimed her innocent."

"Well fairies are infallible judges of character."

"Wipe that smug look off your face."

"What's really eating you? Surely seeing one prisoner saved from execution wouldn't irritate you this much." Steele grumbled and flopped into the nearest chair. "Oh, now I see. Hyron made you responsible for her, is that it?" Steele groaned. Ouji laughed.

"It's not funny."

"To get the joke, I guess you'd have to not be you."

"Ouji, you filed an appeal, but her sentence was already being carried out. What good would it have done?"

He shook his head. "There's no way to tell. Sometimes I win, most times I lose. Even when I do win, it only buys them another week or so."

"Death by torture is designed to be a long and miserable process. Do you ever think your appeals only play right into the Sages' hands?"

"It's sick. I don't like that prisoners have to suffer through it, but if they have the will to live, they can usually last the three days its takes to review evidence."

"Tell me straight Ouji and I swear to you, whatever you say, it won't leave this room."

"Believe what you will, but I didn't do it. I filed an appeal on her behalf and turned in my medical report to contest the results of the forgery."

"You're certain that's all you did?"

"Haven't I told you before, you can't fight a battle against corruption playing by the same twisted rules. I always deal outside the realm of scrutiny."

"Well if you weren't the one who paid for her freedom, than who did?"

"That seems to be the mystery doesn't it?"

Steele dropped his head into his hands. "Who would buy her out of prison, of all people? And why?"

"If nothing else, that should be obvious." Ouji said as he cut the sandwich and offered Steele half.

"Well don't keep me in suspense inspector." He bit into the toasted bread. It crunched loudly and a light dusting of crumbs rained onto his lap.

"What would Daphne, a girl with no technical knowledge and possibly no magical talent have to offer?"

"I don't know."

"Think Steele."

"I honestly can't say."

"And you call yourself a hunter." Ouji dipped the corner of his sandwich into his coffee and took a bite. "You figure out what makes Daphne special and you'll be one step closer to figuring out who saved her and what they plan to do with her."

"You know don't you?"

Ouji shrugged and took another bite of his sandwich. "I have a theory."

"Do you plan on sharing it with the class?"

"Are you ever going to learn to knock?" Steele shoved the remainder of the sandwich in his mouth. He gave Ouji a quick two-finger salute and let the metal doors slide closed behind him.

CHAPTER 15

Checking out of the hospital in this world was just as long and annoying a process as it was on Earth. They told her she'd be out by 1200 hours, yet it took about four hours longer. The nurse removed Daphne's IV, told her she'd be right back and took more than three hours to return with her paperwork and a pair of soft cotton slippers to wear home.

"After a few hours in a place like this, I go stir crazy," Kember said. "I'm sure after a week here, you're happy to be free. It's always nice to be able to sleep in your own bed."

Except I'm not going to sleep in my own bed, Daphne thought. She didn't speak as she followed the blonde into the elevator. At this point, sleeping in her own bed was more of an aspiration than a reality.

They stepped outside into the warm afternoon sun. Kember gently took her by the arm and guided her along the crowded sidewalk. To Daphne the architecture and people's clothing didn't match the technological era. The building facades were intricate works of art. Filigree reached upward like ivy along the sides of Skyscrapers. Gargoyles and scroll designs brought a majestic quality to each building.

The people they passed were dressed in fashions reminiscent of the fifteenth and nineteenth century with a few modern twists. Skirts weren't as bulky and ranged in length from floor length to mini dress. Every piece of clothing was perfectly tailored and accessories provided a brief glimpse into a person's level of wealth. Daphne tensed up as she wondered just how thin and see through her execution dress was.

"Here we are," Kember chimed. She led Daphne into a parking garage that looked more like a torpedo bay. Kember pressed a gold coin into the valet's hand and he helped usher Daphne into the car. The machine looked much like her mother's SUV. It was a mid-sized vehicle with an aerodynamic design. It was gray with a glittery pink racing stripe painted down the center of the chassis.

"It doesn't have any wheels." Daphne blurted out.

"Why would it need wheels?" the valet asked.

"Never mind," Daphne said shaking her head and shrugging. "It was just a stupid observation." Kember chuckled and leaned down to buckle her in. She got in on the driver's side and both doors closed automatically.

"Home."

The engine revved to life and Daphne's stomach flipped as the vehicle tilted backward. There was a sound like a starting gun being fired and the car lurched into the air.

"Take off is a bit rough. Remind me to have the shocks checked."

"Um, sure."

"I was talking to the—"

"Okay," the onboard computer chimed. "I'll remind you."

Kember chuckled softly. "Don't be nervous. Just relax."

Daphne slowly relaxed her grip on the sides of the chair. The indentations left by her fingernails quickly faded. "So, where do you live? And why am I going home with you?"

"My house is in an area outside of town. It's a little isolated, but I think you'll enjoy the peace. I know we do. As for why I'm taking you home with me, let's just say you have a better chance if you have someone to look after you."

"What do you get out of it?"

"I'm sorry?"

"What's in it for you if you take me home? Does the government pay you or what?"

"I don't get anything out of it."

"Then why do it?"

"It's complicated."

"In other words, you have to take me."

"It's temporary, if that's any consolation. I'm sure you'll be able to go home soon."

Daphne sighed. She knew Kember was trying to be nice. It was obvious she was trying to hide the truth from her. *The truth is probably that I'll never be able to go home,* Daphne thought miserably. *I could very well be stuck here for the rest of my life.*

"How fast does this thing go?" Daphne asked, changing the subject to take her mind off all the dark thoughts threatening to overtake her.

"I think this model can break the sound barrier. Of course, we're not going nearly that fast. We have the whole day in front of us, so I'm not in a hurry. We can go faster if you're up for it."

"No, I'm fine." The car sliced through clouds and sped smoothly through the air. She looked out the window and watched the cars speeding below them. Every vehicle moved through the air with the elegance of dolphins in water.

The car eased to the ground. The computer panels in the vehicle slowly powered off and the doors swooshed upward. She had the feeling of being in a less than luxury model of the Lamborghini. Kember unbuckled Daphne's seatbelt and sprang from the car. She spun her key ring on her fingers. Daphne watched Kember glide up the three short steps to the small front porch. She seemed to float over the steps and land on the tiny porch.

She put her key in the lock and the door hinges creaked. She held the door open. Daphne exited the car and nervously crossed the yard. She peered inside the darkened living room before stepping across the threshold. Kember eased in behind her. The door swung closed. As it slammed shut, the lights flickered on. Kember stood in the middle of the floor and waited patiently as Daphne did a slow turn and took in her new surroundings.

"How did you—"

"Some parts of the house are computerized. You'll get used to how the lights work in a few days."

"Okay."

"I'm sorry. I should have realized," she hesitated. "Everything here is strange to you."

"It's fine."

"Why don't you have a seat? I'm sure you're dying for something other than hospital food."

Kember disappeared behind a wall. Daphne slowly walked around the room and ran her hands along the walls and furniture. The black fabric sofa was placed in front of a large flat screen television and the beige painted walls were made of drywall. The place was clean and well organized. The square patterned rug and other modern accents added splashes of color to the space. The colors yellow, turquoise and peacock green in the rug were carried throughout the space by pillows and vases of fresh flowers.

Kember returned with a serving tray. The green ceramic tea pot gave off a scent that reminded Daphne of Pillsbury cinnamon rolls. Kember set the tray on the glass coffee table and filled three cups.

"Why three?" she asked.

"I don't exactly live alone." Kember stated.

"Oh, so you have a roommate?"

"Please sit down. Let me try to explain things before he gets here."

"Before who gets here?"

"How much do you remember about how you ended up here? The shock chamber has a tendency to damage brain cells."

"Well, I don't really know where here is, but I haven't forgotten anything. I've been dreaming about the whole thing for days. Every time I close my eyes I just keep praying that when I open them, I'll wake up and this will all have been some really crazy dream." Daphne politely accepted the cup and took a seat on the couch beside Kember. "I was shopping for school clothes with my parents when the roof caved in. This guy destroyed the ceiling and grabbed me without even touching me. He kept saying that my reign of terror was over and he was going to bring me to justice."

"I see." Kember looked down at her fingers and nibbled on the inside of her lip.

"It's him, isn't it?"

She looked up at Daphne in surprise. The look on her face was like that of a deer caught in car headlights.

"Your roommate, the third cup. He lives here! What is this, some kind of sick joke?"

"Daphne, please try to calm down."

"I shouldn't have to live like this, constantly being watched by some conviction happy lunatic. I haven't done anything wrong. I was taken from my family and my home. I've been beaten, I've been tortured and I almost died because of him. I'm the victim here."

"You have every reason to hate the person responsible for your situation. But—"

"You're right, I do. You don't know how many times I wanted to scream and cry. But I didn't because I kept hearing my mother's voice in my head. Crying doesn't solve anything, it just wastes time."

"Your mother's a very wise woman."

"Please, just let me go home."

"I'm afraid that won't be possible," Steele said. He stood in the doorway. Daphne's rage exploded. She let out a frustrated scream. He didn't flinch as a hot cup of tea soared too far left of his head. The cup clattered onto the porch. Tea splattered over the walls and floors.

"You!"

"Daphne please," Kember pleaded, positioning herself between Daphne and Steele.

"This is your fault. And now you're refusing to take me home. They let me go. Can't you accept that you were wrong?"

"No."

"Steele, you're not helping," Kember hissed.

"I should have put two and two together. No wonder you took such good care of me. You obviously feel guilty."

"I am on your side," Kember said defensively. "Unfortunately, Steele is right. You can't go home. At least, not yet."

"Why not? He brought me here didn't he? He should be able to take me back. And I want to go back."

"Inter-dimensional travel isn't that simple." Kember continued. "It takes a lot of energy and frankly a lot of luck to guarantee safe arrival at your destination. To improve our chances, we rely on natural portals within the space-time continuum."

"Portals?"

"I believe you call them wormholes."

"Okay, so where's the nearest wormhole?"

"The wormhole which enabled Steele to bring you here has a recurring cycle. It opens at regular intervals for a limited period of time and then closes again. Do you understand what I'm saying?"

"You're saying I have to wait for the wormhole to open again."

"Yes, that's it exactly."

"How long? How long do I have to wait?" Kember looked to Steele for an answer. He sighed and retrieved the mug from the porch. He closed the front door and crossed the room, making sure to keep at least three feet between Daphne and himself. He positioned his body to ensure he was always facing her.

"Five years," he said quietly.

Daphne's shoulders drooped. "Five years? I can't stay here for that long. I have school and my parents. What about my parents? What about me? What's going to happen to me?"

"You'll live here until then," Steele finished.

"I don't want to live here," Daphne replied angrily. Her voice trembled and cracked.

"Well that's good because I don't want you to live here." Steele grumbled.

"Steele!" Kember hissed in his direction. She turned back to Daphne. "What Steele means to say is we're responsible for you until we can take you home. And we're more than happy to have you. Isn't that right?"

"I'm going upstairs," Steele responded.

"Daphne." Kember placed a hand on her shoulder. Daphne looked up at her through tear blurred eyes. "I know it's not what you were hoping for, but I'm sure we can make the most of the situation. Five years is a long time after all."

"Yeah."

Daphne reached up and took the gold cross in her hands. Her eyes filled with tears. *This isn't fair. This just isn't fair.* The words kept echoing in her head. *By some miracle I get saved from death and I end up in the last place I wanted to be. Please, just let me wake up from this nightmare.*

"Five years." She said the words aloud. She repeated the words several times. Her tongue felt like it was made of cotton. No matter how many times she said them, the words didn't make the situation any less surreal.

Daphne's head snapped up. The sound of clanging metal and broken glass startled her. She rubbed her eyes. "I must have fallen asleep." She rose to her feet and headed toward the kitchen. She found Kember cradling her bleeding hand against her chest. Shards of glass were scattered over the floor.

"Be careful," Kember warned.

"What happened?"

"It's nothing. I can handle it."

"Let me help you." Daphne found a towel and wrapped Kember's injured arm. She gathered the pots and pans and set them on the countertop.

"There's a broom in that closet."

Daphne followed the direction of Kember's finger. She reached out and the door seemed to vanish. She jerked her hand back and then breathed a sigh of relief. She retrieved the broom and quickly swept the floor. She was careful to go over each of the floor tiles twice. As a kid, she could remember stepping on almost invisible pieces of glass weeks after breaking something.

"Do you want some help?"

"You're the guest. At least on your first day here I should cook for you."

"It's okay. I know my way around a kitchen." She hesitated as she took in the pristine space. Polished metal and tile surfaces gleamed in the artificial light. "Or maybe not." She recognized the sink and something that looked like a microwave. Kember laughed. "Which of these silver things is the fridge, and which one is the stove?"

Kember shook her head. "Really, I just need to bandage this cut."

"I'm pretty smart. Just talk me through it."

"Alright, if you insist." Even though Daphne wasn't thrilled with her situation, she was hungry. And she was desperate for something other than soup and crackers. The hospital nutritionist had provided her with a variety of well-balanced, yet tasteless meals. The only thing that'd been worth eating were the chilled berries floating in her water glass.

Steele lowered himself in the tub until the hot water reached his chin. He closed his eyes and tried to let the heat ease his tension. His muscles relaxed, but he was unable to clear his mind. He played through the conversation with the Guild Master in his head. He'd argued until he was hoarse. *What else could I have said to convince him to pawn her off on someone else?*

"This is ridiculous. Hyron can't really expect me to babysit for the next five years. There's got to be a way out of this."

He groaned. Then there was the conversation he'd had with Ouji. He'd teleported aboard the Templar ship to confront his old friend about the girl being pardoned from execution. While the doctor swore his hands were clean, Steele wasn't entirely sure he believed that the doctor hadn't paid her ransom.

"Of course," he reminded himself, "there's always the chance that he's telling the truth. And if that's the case, who else would want her?"

Until recently the sorceress Katz controlled a large portion of the criminal element. Those who followed her did so out of a weird combination of fear, respect, and individual feelings of loyalty. Since her arrest, he was aware of the battle for power in the underworld. Could they be hoping to recruit Daphne into their ranks? And if they did, how useful could she really be? If she was indeed an innocent double from the alternate reality, she brought no value to a well-established team of seasoned felons.

"It has to be something else." His voice echoed across the surface of the water. "What does Ouji know that I don't?" Steele shook his head and growled. He dipped his head into the warm soapy water. Don't assume too much, he told himself mentally. Ouji's good at pretending to know more than he really does.

He leapt to his feet when he heard the crash. Water sloshed onto the floor. He slipped on the water coated tile. He threw open the door and raced toward the kitchen. Steele was halfway down the stairs before it dawned on him that he and Kember were no longer alone. He dashed up the stairs and yanked a thick towel from the rack by the door.

He hurried to the kitchen and stopped just before he reached the archway. He listened as Kember gave instructions. Each instruction was answered either with the sound of chopping or a young girl asking, "Is this it?" Using the mirrors he'd strategically placed on the living room walls, he could see Kember perched on the countertop as Daphne diced vegetables and sliced meat like a professional. He took a stepped forward as he watched Kember unwrap a towel and clean her bleeding arm in the sink.

She positioned herself slightly behind Daphne and looked in his direction. She shook her head and waved him away. He ducked out of sight seconds before Daphne glanced over her shoulder. Kember flashed her a smile and used her body as a shield as Steele slinked back up the stairs. He could hear Kember praising the quality of Daphne's work. Back in the bathroom, he let the water out of the tub and half-heartedly dried the bathroom floor.

"I don't like this," he said to himself. "That girl is trouble."

CHAPTER 16

Daphne opened her eyes and breathed a sigh of relief to find everything the way she'd left it. Her bed was against the left wall, positioned just beneath the edge of the windowsill. Under the window was her desk and laptop. The white lights from the laptop flashed to show it was still charging. Across from her was a single bookcase over piled with science fiction books, fantasy novels and manga. Above her overflowing shelf were two floating cube shelves which held her growing collection of anime and the drafts of her screenplay.

She glanced upward and squealed into her pillow. The silvery glow of a single moon was a welcome site. She rolled onto her back and ran her fingers through her hair. The smell of bacon coming from downstairs was the icing on the cake. Regrettably, the aroma woke her empty stomach. It gurgled as the smell intensified. The image of her bedroom began to fade.

Daphne rolled onto her side and squeezed her eyes tighter. She desperately wanted to stay asleep. "Please, please, please," she screamed inside her head, "please let me be home." Even before she opened her eyes, she knew the wish was wasted. She sighed as she gazed through the window up into the purplish blue glow of the planet's double moons.

"I should just give up," she told herself. She pulled the sheets to her face and allowed her tears to soak into the fabric. She sat up and looked at her room again. It was about the same size as her room on Earth. The bed was against the same wall. Beneath the window, where her desk would have been was a cushioned bench. And instead of a bookshelf, the far wall had a tortoise shell accent table. Instead of books, it held a porcelain vase of budding flowers.

Daphne yawned and stretched. She could hear Kember calling her name. The woman's footsteps were as silent as a ninja's. She moved so quickly and quietly that Daphne jumped in surprise when she looked up and saw her standing in the doorway with clothes draped over her arm.

"Good morning." She sang with a broad smile.

"It's still dark out," Daphne grumbled.

"I know but it's already 10."

"Then why is it so dark?" she yawned.

"This planet is larger than yours. It takes a while to make a complete revolution around the sun. Also, there are the two moons. Oh, and we're on a 36 hour day."

"What? 36 hours? You can't be serious."

Kember ran her finger along the edge of the wall and the lights kicked on. Daphne squinted and shielded her eyes until they adjusted to the brightness. She grumbled, yawned again and rubbed her eyes.

"Come on, we've got a busy day today."

"Where're we going?"

"Shopping."

"Seriously?"

"You don't want to spend the rest of your life in prison robes do you?" Daphne shook her head. "I didn't think so. Here, I brought you something of mine. It might be a little big, but it should work until we get a chance to see the tailor."

"Thanks."

"No problem. Get dressed and come downstairs. Breakfast is almost ready."

Daphne hadn't realized how tall Kember was until she tried on the dress she'd loaned her. On its rightful owner, the dress probably would have stopped just above the knee. On Daphne it came to her ankles. She laughed and tossed the leggings on the bed. There was no point in bothering to try them on.

"At least we wear the same size shoes." Daphne said to herself. "Well, almost."

Kember's feet were about a half size smaller than Daphne's. The worn leather of the boots gave easily to accommodate her toes. The sole of the shoes had been worn so thin she could feel the unevenness of the wooden floors. Kember was waiting for her at the bottom of the stairs.

Kember's laugh was light and musical. She shook her head in amusement. Tears pooled in the corners of her eyes.

"I'm glad you're enjoying this." Daphne said sarcastically.

"I'm sorry, you just look so cute."

Daphne shook her head and rolled her eyes. "When does the sun come up?"

"The sun should be up in about an hour or so. I made an appointment with the head seamstress of the Dawn Needles Guild. I think she has a few things in stock that you might like. It shouldn't take her too long to put you in something that fits."

"Wait, are everybody's clothes custom made?"

"Isn't that the case on your world?"

"No. We go to the mall."

"Mall? What's a mall?"

"It's a big place with a bunch of different stores in it. You go from store to store and you buy what you like. It's fast, easy and no tailors. Steele's practically an expert. He destroyed one."

"Hmm. Interesting concept, but sorry, no malls. Here we have guilds. Every city or town has at least one local branch. And each branch is managed by a larger main guild. They regulate how many branches per town, handle customer complaints and any disputes between local branches."

"That sounds like a complicated way of doing things."

"Um, how can I put this? Oh! On some worlds, um, planets, they have corporations. A guild is sort of like that. You've got a headquarters in one place and then every local branch is like a store in a chain."

"Oh, I get it. So, then are jobs handed down through families? Like does someone become a healer because the rest of their family members are healers?"

"No. Well, sometimes. Children go to school for a while to learn how to read and other basic things. Then, when they're about your age, they choose a guild and apply to become an apprentice. If accepted, they'll work under a master, someone who has already completed apprenticeship and now works and earns a salary as a member of the guild. They study and work under the master for several years in exchange for training and room and board. Once they graduate and become guild members, they have to work for three years and give half their salary to the guild to pay the actual cost of their education and lodging."

"So, they're indentured servants?"

"That's one way to put it. We prefer to think of it as taking out a loan. Only money doesn't change hands up front and there's usually no interest."

"What happens if someone really hates their job?"

"After you've paid off your apprentice debts, you're free to choose another guild and start the process over."

"Don't you people go to college?"

"I think universities were tried in some provinces in the past, but at the end of their education, most people didn't have any practical knowledge and skills. There was still some hands-on training needed. People thought it better to learn from experienced guild members."

"What about advancements in technology and —"

"Guilds are good about sharing that sort of information with their members. Trust me the system isn't as complex as it seems on the surface."

"If you say so." Daphne sat down and nibbled on a piece of bacon. "What guild do you belong to?"

"I don't belong to a guild. My situation is a little different from the average citizen."

"Oh yeah? How so?"

"Just eat. We don't want to keep the madam waiting. She doesn't usually work on eighth days, but I convinced her to do it as a personal favor to me."

"Okay, okay. I can take a hint." Daphne was burning with questions. While she was glad to be rid of the execution gown, she was a little nervous about going to the seamstress. Her last shopping trip hadn't ended like it should have.

"You lying sack of—"

"Good morning to you too Steele," Guild Master Hyron said sarcastically.

"Do you know what this is?" Steele snapped as he brandished a thick brown envelope.

"No, but it looks official." Hyron folded his newspaper and laid it on the desk.

"It's a notification of inquiry."

"Hmm. Sounds serious."

"My entire life is going to be scrutinized. There will be a solicitor in my house, going through my records, my finances. I'm to be questioned."

"So?"

"Wipe that smirk off your face. This is your fault."

"How so?"

"I believe your exact words were you're just a scapegoat. It's only on paper. There's nothing to worry about."

"I also told you that I'm not in the business of fixing guild member's messes." Steele threw the envelope. It flopped against Hyron's chest. The guild master handled the envelope carefully. He slowly opened it and read the letter. "Sounds to me like you didn't pay your bribe."

"And why would I?"

"It's the way of the world son."

"I've never paid a bribe in my life and I don't intend to start now. And don't call me son."

The guild master shrugged. "I'm afraid I can't help you. It's already been stamped by a Sage from the high court." He stuffed the letter back into the envelope and tossed it onto the desk. It slid across the surface and teetered on the edge. Steele snatched it up and tucked it inside his jacket.

"So what am I supposed to do?"

Hyron leaned back and propped his feet up on his desk. Lacing his fingers together, he cradled the back of his head. "You go through with the inquiry of course."

"This is ridiculous."

"You're overreacting."

"I could lose my license."

"Just relax. You're a good hunter and you're honest. You keep a level head and you don't have anything to hide, which is something I can't say about most others in this business or this guild for that matter. Follow procedure and you'll be fine."

Steele grumbled and turned to leave.

"Oh, one more thing," Hyron said.

"What?"

"I should warn you, I've filed a petition to have Daphne added as Realms Honor's first apprentice."

"You really have lost it, haven't you?"

"It's called damage control."

"I refuse to share trade secrets with that wolf in sheep's clothing. I know she's guilty."

"Of what?"

"She's not as innocent as everyone else seems to think."

"Well if you think she's guilty of something, having her around will make it easier to catch her in the act, don't you think?" Steele mumbled in dissent. "The fact of the matter is you're the reason Daphne is in our dimension. Therefore you are legally responsible for her care until she can be returned safely. So either you become her legal guardian and let her sponge off you for the next half decade, or you can become her master and train her to be a hunter."

"I don't like it. We know nothing about this girl, who or what she really is. And you want to share trade secrets?"

"Trust me on this Steele. Children are worse than leeches. They eat your food and they're a drain on your wallet and your sanity. Put her to work and make her earn her keep."

"Even if I did, I can't say she'll be much use. She speaks the language well enough, but she can't read runes."

"Get her a tutor. Doesn't that wizard friend of yours have an apprentice who's looking for a side job?"

"It's bad enough that Kember took my wallet and the girl and went shopping for new clothes. There's no way I'm paying for a tutor."

Hyron laughed. "As cheap as ever. Don't worry," he said lowering his feet to the floor. "I'll pay the boy's fee and give you a finder's bonus if you make the arrangements. Sound good?"

"I suppose. It's not as if I really have a say in the matter." Steele said resignedly.

Hyron breathed a sigh of relief and tried to sound gruff as he hid a smile. "Good. Now get out of my office." Steele turned again to leave. As he crossed the threshold Hyron called out to him. "Oh Steele?"

"What now?"

"Give this to the kid will you? As a token of our friendship." He tossed a tiny velour bag in his direction. Steele held out his hands and caught the cinch sack by its thin ribbon strings. He looked up at Hyron to ask a question, but the office door swooshed closed with a loud snap.

CHAPTER 17

Daphne stood with her arms air planed out. Madam Pietryson circled her several times, taking measurements and muttering. She draped different fabrics on Daphne. If there was something she liked, the madam would tear the material into strips and pin them around Daphne's body in different curves and lines. She would nod or make faces as her apprentice took pictures of Daphne from every possible angle. She would then remove the pins and drop the strips into a woven grass basket on the floor. This continued until she made a gesture and the apprentice disappeared behind a curtain. During this process, Kember politely commented on the seamstress's displayed designs.

"This one's adorable," she said about a black and white shirt dress. "Don't you think so Daphne?"

At first glance the piece looked like it was made from a simple hounds tooth print. A closer inspection revealed that the design had been created by sewing individual strips of fabric together. The collar had been embellished with clear crystals and it had been accessorized with a beaded belt.

"It's gorgeous. It reminds me of something my mother would wear."

The seamstress almost choked on a pin as she stifled down a laugh. "That's one of my apprentice's creations."

"For your apprentice to create something so beautiful, it certainly speaks volumes to your level of talent and creativity as a master." Kember gushed.

"You can put your arms down now," the madam instructed Daphne. She lowered her arms and carefully stepped down from the small circular platform. "Have a look around the shop. Let me know if you see anything you like. If you don't, feel free to take a look at these." She handed Daphne a thin sketchbook. She bowed and disappeared into the back room.

Unlike most of the places she'd seen, the madam's shop was very mundane. The wooden door had a brass knob and there was a tiny metal bell above the door which jingled to alert her whenever a customer came and went. There weren't any light fixtures or outlets. Instead, the shop had large picture windows. The seamstress still had the curtains drawn, but light streamed in from tiny triangular sky lights. Sitting on her main counter was a ledger and an inkpot with a quill sticking out of it.

"Does the Madam have something against electricity?" Daphne asked quietly.

"Many in the tailors guild do. For them, clothing is more than just a necessity. It's a form of art. Some even feel that technology will lead to the destruction of society and values."

"But that's crazy."

"Is it?" the seamstress asked, reentering the shop. "While it's true that technology has benefits, it also has its downfalls. There's pollution, the garbage manufacturing creates, and let's not forget what men do with weapons."

"I guess. But I mean, look at this place. Compared to where I'm from, this planet is millennia ahead. This world has stuff people only dream about."

"Every invention started as a dream. It's what we do when our dreams become reality that makes the difference. Well now, see anything that catches your eye?"

"Umm…" Daphne paced the room again. There wasn't anything that really stood out. The items were beautiful, but more sophisticated than anything she could see herself wearing hanging around Steele and Kember's house. She opened the sketchbook and flipped through the pages. "Everything in here," she said, handing the book back to the seamstress.

The seamstress smiled and gestured for Daphne to follow her. Behind the counter were two barstools. Madam Pietryson leaned against the wooden counter and gestured for Daphne and Kember to have a seat. She handed Daphne a scrap of paper and pushed the ink pot toward her. Pietryson turned to Kember.

"What's the budget?"

"Something for every day of the week and something formal."

"Shoes and undergarments as well?"

"Of course."

"Any accessories?"

"Use your discretion."

"Well little one that gives you a total of 11 out of 37."

"11? I thought there were only seven days in a week."

The seamstress and Kember exchanged looks. "Eight days in a week, one formal piece, and something to wear home today, makes 11." The seamstress winked.

"Oh." Daphne nodded in understanding.

Eight plus one and one made ten, but the woman was giving her something extra. Daphne slowly turned the pages and carefully scrutinized each colored sketch. When she was finished, she handed the list to the seamstress. The woman's eyebrows went up in surprise and she wrinkled her nose as she stared at the page. She looked from Daphne to Kember, mumbled an unfamiliar phrase and the lines on the page shifted and twisted.

Daphne could no longer recognize her own handwriting. The symbols on the page were completely foreign to her. The madam thumbed through the pages and used the pictures to double check the girl's choices. Kember counted amethyst crusted gold coins onto the counter. The seamstress nodded in approval and quickly scrawled a receipt. She blew on the ink to help it dry.

"Come by around closing. I'm sure I'll have something ready for you."

Kember nodded, hopped gracefully off the stool and glided toward the door. Before leaving she turned and bowed to the seamstress. Daphne followed Kember's example. The tiny bell chimed their departure as the door swung shut.

Now that the sun was up, the streets were starting to come to life. Shops were opening and a few people were out trying to get an early start on their day. Overhead a few flying cars zipped by. They walked to a cross walk and waited while a hovering motorcycle and bus passed.

"Can she really sew all that by hand in a day?"

Kember's laughed rang out into the street. People cast curious looks in their direction. She tossed her blonde hair and it danced in the breeze caused by the passing vehicles. The strands floated slowly like dandelion seeds. Her hair landed softly on her shoulders without a single hair out of place.

"Don't let that act fool you. She's got three apprentices and a sewing machine hidden in the back room, and her apartment is state of the art."

"But her shop doesn't even have lights."

"That's to keep up appearances with the guild. They're very strict about clothing craft being an art."

"I guess that explains why her assistant had a digital camera. But who cares if the work gets done a little faster so long as it gets done?"

"Let me ask you this. If you saw a beautiful marble sculpture and found out the artist used a laser and a computer instead of a chisel, would you still find it as spectacular?"

"Not really."

"Why?"

"Because he didn't do anything. He just pushed a button."

"Exactly." The light changed from orange to yellow. As they crossed the street Daphne couldn't shake the feeling that she was being watched.

"Kember," Daphne hissed. She moved closer to her escort. She accidently stepped on the woman's heels.

"Ouch."

"Sorry. It's just, is it me or are people staring?"

"This way."

Kember glanced over her shoulder and wrapped an arm around Daphne's shoulders. She guided her into a small shop. The air smelled heavily of coffee and pastries. She chose a table in the corner farthest from the door. The waiter brought a menu and two complementary scones.

"Could I see a copy of today's scroll please?"

"Of course my lady." He bowed respectfully at Kember but eyed Daphne with a mix of terror and suspicion.

"See?"

"Here you are." Their server stood as far back from Daphne and the table as he could. His hands trembled as he held the newspaper outward.

"Thank you," Kember said as she took the paper. The waiter scrambled away and ducked into the kitchen. "This might explain a few things." She slid the newspaper across the table. Daphne's mouth dropped open.

"Is that my face?" A large picture of her was on the front page. Beside it was a picture of Diamara Katz.

"Yes."

"What's it say?"

"Just details of your arrest, the trial and the circumstances surrounding your release."

"Okay. What circumstances?"

"They confirm that you were taken by mistake. However, they claim that while you may not be the sorceress Katz, you have some connection with her and are currently under investigation."

"Is that true? Is that why they're making me live with Steele?"

"No. It's not like that at all. The daily scroll is plagued with half-truths. You can never be sure what part of this rag is gossip, truth or paid propaganda."

"But don't people believe what they read? I mean, where I come from the press is valued for their objectivity and honesty."

"I'm not going to lie to you. Most people won't care what this thing says. The story could have touted your innocence. Still, there are people who will take one look at your face and refuse to make the distinction between you and her."

"But she looks nothing like me."

"She's your alternate self."

"So? She's so old. I mean look at the lines around her eyes and the wrinkles on her forehead. And then she has all these crazy tattoos on her neck. I would never get a tattoo. They're so tacky."

"Needless to say, most people won't bother to make the distinction, or try."

"Are you telling me that I'm going to spend the next five years as public enemy number one?"

Kember nodded.

"I don't believe this. So people are either gonna be afraid of me or try to kill me?"

"I'm afraid so."

"This sucks. What am I supposed to do?"

"Buy a hat?"

Daphne laughed. She shook her head. A hat and a pair of oversized sunglasses didn't help celebrities on Earth hide from the paparazzi. If anything, a disguise made you look even more conspicuous.

They returned to the seamstress's shop after a full day of shopping. The bell chimed as they entered. Madam Pietryson was waiting for them. She clapped her hands. In reaction to the sound, the shop door locked and all the curtains drew themselves closed. She looked Daphne up and down and smirked.

"I see you've been reading the Daily Scroll," she said, ushering her back onto the platform. In anticipation of their arrival, the seamstress had put up a three sided mirror. She whisked a dress from behind the counter and held it up for inspection. "Well what do you think?"

"My mom always says you have to try things on."

"Well, go on."

Daphne slipped out of Kember's ill-fitting dress and stepped into the one the seamstress had designed for her. It was a blue and green mini dress with three quarter sleeves and cut-out shoulders.

"It's cute. I like it. Very retro." She took off the hat and shook her curls. "It's perfect."

"Not quite," the madam said smiling. She wrapped a black belt around Daphne's waist. It fit perfectly. "I only give a couple inches of extra room, so don't get fat."

"Is this magic fabric?" Kember asked fingering the material.

"Yes, 100 percent in the belt and 40 percent in the dress. It's essential for hidden pockets. Only the best for the exclusive Realms Honor's first apprentice."

"What's Realms Honor?" Daphne asked, turning to the side and looking over her shoulder.

"It's Steele's guild," Kember said.

"Membership has always been by invitation only. You're very lucky to be accepted as an apprentice," the seamstress added.

"You must be mistaken," Kember said. "She's not—"

"Apparently you haven't read the afternoon edition of the Daily Scroll." She held her hand up and the newspaper materialized out of thin air. "Hyron made an official statement."

"I don't believe this," Kember breathed. She scanned the page a second and third time.

"Wait, who's Hyron?" Daphne asked.

"Daphne, we're going." She snapped. The tips of her ears were flushed.

"Okay." She stepped down from the platform and bowed to the seamstress. Kember stormed from the shop with the newspaper gripped firmly in her hand. The tiny bell chimed as the shop door slammed.

CHAPTER 18

"What the frell is Hyron smoking?" Kember shouted. The flush on her ears had crept down the side of her head to her neck. She threw the newspaper at Steele. It bounced off his chest and landed on the sofa next to him.

"I thought you didn't read that dribble." Steele replied nonchalantly.

"Would you mind separating fact from fiction for me?"

"He thinks I should make Daphne my apprentice."

"It's a stupid idea. No offense dear," she said to Daphne before turning back to Steele.

"None taken."

"There's not an ounce of muscle on her, she doesn't have a mean bone in her body and the child can't even read simple Runey."

"Hyron's agreed to pay for a tutor."

"A tutor? You can't be serious. Hyron's cheaper than you are. I've never known him to volunteer to pay for anything in his life."

"It's all arranged. I stopped by Wizards Portal earlier today."

"You spoke to Hilia?"

"I did. He agreed to loan out his apprentice. Marcus can handle reading, writing and basic magic. I'm sure that'll keep her busy."

"Have you given any thought to what happens if she actually excels at her training?"

"Nope, can't say that I have."

"Steele, look at her. She's not capable of killing."

"Excuse me, what?" Daphne cut in.

"Sweetheart, I'm sorry, but could you go to your room?"

"Uh, sure," Daphne responded nervously.

"Don't bother," Steele said, rising to his feet. "I'll leave."

"Steele—"

"My hands are tied. The law is very clear."

"But Steele, she's likely to get herself killed."

"The fact of the matter is we can't afford to just feed her for the next five years. I'm responsible for her, so I can't just pawn her off on another guild member. We're stuck with her, so she may as well make herself useful."

"Funny, that sounds like something Hyron would say."

"Excuse me but don't I get a say in this?" Daphne asked.

"By all means," Steele said as he dog-eared the page of the book he'd been reading and tucked it under his arm.

"I'm sorry you feel like I'm so much trouble, but this is your fault. You don't want me here and I don't want to be here. I should be at home studying for the SAT's and thinking about colleges and my future. Instead I'm stuck God knows where. I don't know anybody, I don't know anything and I'm at the mercy of strangers."

"Is there a point to this?"

"My point is I don't want to be a hired gun or do whatever it is you do. I can earn my keep. I can cook; I can clean or do laundry or whatever else is expected of me. I will bide my time and stay out of your way. But I just want to go home. And when I do, I don't want to look back feeling like I owed you anything."

"I'm sure your parents filled your head will all sorts of inspirational crap, so let me be the first to tell you how things are. Life isn't fair and we don't always get what we want. The rules here are very different and the sooner you accept that, the better off you'll be."

"But there has to be some other way," Kember tried to argue.

"Marcus will be here tomorrow." Steele shifted his book to his other arm and headed for the stairs. "Hey kid. Before I forget, here." he said. He tossed her the sack Hyron had given him earlier. He retreated up stairs with Kember trailing behind him, the tips of her ears still blazing red. The sight made Daphne smile. In a weird way they remind her of her own parents.

They disappeared and Daphne headed into the kitchen. While they were out, Kember had picked up a few groceries. While they were shopping she'd explained to Daphne the difference between the fruits and the vegetables. She'd also purchased a produce marker and drawn a star on the veggies. One thing Daphne had learned during her time in the hospital was that even if something looked similar, it didn't always cook or taste the same as it did on

Earth. She didn't really feel like putting any effort into the task, so she turned on the oven. While it pre-heated, she emptied the contents of the black sack onto the counter.

The handful of cash she'd had in her pockets minus the change, her watch and the touch screen mp3 player spilled out. The watch clasp had been repaired, yet the music player battery was almost dead. She browsed through her playlist. She couldn't help but laugh as she shook her head in disbelief. She scrolled through the music listed. It had all been completely rearranged. Daphne turned the bag inside out, but it was empty. Her ear bud headphones were gone.

"At least I got most of my stuff back. I wonder what they did with my clothes," she said aloud. The sound of her voice in the empty kitchen made the place feel emptier. Daphne sighed. "What a day."

She washed her hands and sorted through Steele and Kember's meager supply of bake ware until she found a pot deep enough for the roast. She could already hear Steele's voice in the back of her head lecturing her for cooking dinner so early in the day.

"This place is crazy. Up before the sun, 36 hour days and now the next five years of my life have already been decided for me? It's the law. What a crock. I bet it's all something they cooked up together. Kember's definitely in on it. They're never going let me leave here."

"Talking to yourself?" Steele asked. Daphne jumped. She hadn't heard him come back down the stairs.

"No. I was just thinking out loud."

"Right." He opened the fridge and grabbed a piece of sliced deli meat and something that looked like a pear.

"I'm not crazy. Talking to yourself is perfectly normal."

"If you say so."

"Why don't you just—" Daphne stopped. She bit her lip and turned back to the roast. If she really was going to be stuck here, pissing Steele off probably wasn't a good idea.

"Why don't I what?" he asked.

"Nothing."

He laughed.

"What's so funny?"

"Nothing." He shoved another piece of meat in his mouth and grabbed two bottles of what looked like water. He closed the refrigerator with his foot and backed out of the kitchen.

Kember's right, Steele thought. No matter how suspicious I am of her, the kid's too mild mannered for this business. She has her moments when her temper flares, proving she's feisty enough, but she goes out of her way to avoid conflict. Could be fear or it could be something else.

"Unless," he mused.

"Unless what? Kember asked as Steele pushed open the bedroom door.

"Unless she's what this is really about."

"What are you going on about now?"

"I was just thinking about something the doctor said about Daphne being here was no accident. That someone meant for me to bring her here."

"Who would have the foresight and ability to set something like this up? It's probably all coincidence."

"What does a double with no magical aptitude and no skills have to offer?"

"Is that supposed to be a riddle?" Kember asked. Steele passed her the pear and a bottle of water. "How should I know? But you have an idea, don't you?"

"I'm thinking that maybe it's not about what she can do; it's about what she will do. This whole thing hinges on me turning her into a hunter. And I'll bet Hyron has his hands in it."

CHAPTER 19

There was a soft knock on the door, a brief pause and more knocking. The door to Daphne's room slowly edged open. Daphne groaned as light from the hall seeped into the room and struck her face. Grumbling, she rolled onto her side and pulled the covers over her head.

"Ugh. Kember," she whined. "It's still dark out."

"Um," a male's voice asked. "It's Daphne isn't it?"

Daphne's heart froze. Her breathing skipped. Calm down, she thought. Maybe you imagined it. Trembling and struggling to make her chest look as if it were barely rising and falling, she opened her eyes and peered from beneath the covers. There was definitely someone standing in her room. She craned her neck to try and get a good look, but with the light behind him, he was shrouded in shadow.

"Who are you?" she asked, her voice quivering.

"I'm Marcus, your tutor."

"Oh." She let her head drop back onto the pillow. She breathed out audibly and felt the tightness in her chest instantly ease. Her heart was still racing, but it was quickly slowing to a more normal pace. "Go away. I'm sick," she said as she pulled the covers back over her face.

Marcus laughed. "I thought Steele told you I was coming."

"He did. So?"

"So, it's time for your lesson."

"I already told you, I'm sick."

"It looks more like you're sleeping in to me."

"Do I look like I care?" He shook his head. "Then go away and come back at a decent hour."

"Sleep, don't sleep. It makes no difference to me. I get paid either way. But I don't think Guild Master Hyron would be happy if he found out he was paying for nothing."

Daphne peeled back the covers and shot Marcus an ugly look. "Well whose fault is that? Not that it's any of your business, but I didn't ask for a tutor."

"Maybe not, but take it from me, you don't want to end up owing a man like Hyron anything. Not that it's any of my business of course."

Daphne sat up and glared at Marcus as she rubbed sleep from one eye. "Look. I'm not here by choice. I'm here against my will and I'm stuck here until I can go home. And not that someone like you really cares, but my only plan is to pass the time. Besides, the way I understand it is that the law says the guild is responsible for me, seeing as how this is their mistake."

"Technically, you're right. But if that portal opens and Hyron feels like you owe him, you won't be going anywhere."

Marcus turned on the lights. She could see him clearly. He had dark auburn hair. It was straight and cut in layers, stopping just below his ears. His nose and cheeks were dotted with freckles and his dark brown eyes were like two deep pools of milk chocolate. He flashed her a smile and Daphne felt her breath catch in her throat. Everything about him was familiar. If it weren't for her circumstances, she'd swear they'd met before.

"You're making this up?" Daphne half asked the declaration.

Marcus shrugged. "I could be. How would you know? You're a stranger here."

"That isn't fair. Tell me; is what you just said true?"

"Could be. Doesn't matter anyway, you're up now aren't you?"

Daphne rolled her eyes. What a dirty trick, she thought bitterly. It's just the sort of Galen would do. She smiled.

"Do I have something on my face?" Marcus asked.

Daphne shook her head. "No. Why?"

"You're smiling and that laugh is kind of sinister," he joked.

"Oh, it's nothing. Anyway, you win. Give me ten minutes."

He took five steps back and closed the door. Daphne crawled out of bed. She moaned a complaint the instant her toes touched the floor. Kember always kept the house cold and Daphne dreaded leaving a warm bed for a virtual freezer almost as much as she hated getting up before the sun. She slipped out of the white execution gown she'd been using for pajamas and put on the mini dress she'd gotten from Madam Pietryson. She combed her fingers through her hair and fished the hand-me-down boots from under the bed. She tucked the mp3 player into the belt. She adjusted the belt to make sure it was tight enough to hold the device in place.

When Daphne opened the door, she found Marcus standing in the hall. He was leaning against the wall with his hands tucked in his pockets. He smiled. Daphne cut her eyes at him. There was no mistaking it: the dimples in his cheeks, that smug smile. He was a dead ringer or Galen.

"What?" he asked.

"Nothing. You just look like someone I know."

"Like a movie star or boyfriend?"

"Ha! Don't flatter yourself."

"It was worth a shot," he said with a shrug.

"So," Daphne asked as they descended the stairs, "what do you know about hidden pockets?"

"That's pretty advanced magic."

"Oh. So, if I'm not diving in head first, what's in the lesson plan?"

"I thought we'd start with something simple."

"Define simple."

"The alphabet."

"You're not serious."

Marcus jumped the last three steps to the living room floor. On the coffee table he'd already spread a collection of books. He sat cross-legged on the floor and patted a space on the rug next to him.

"You do realize I'm wearing a dress?"

"So go change."

"I can't. I don't own anything else." *But I'll bet you already knew that,* Daphne thought cynically. His lips moved as he silently mouthed a string of words. The table rose in height a few inches. He pushed himself up and settled on the couch.

"Better?"

Daphne walked around the table. She ran her fingers around the edges of it. She stooped down and quickly examined the table legs. They were solid. She sat next to Marcus being careful to keep a foot of space between them. She glanced down at the books and papers he'd assembled. *I may as well be looking at an alien language,* Daphne thought miserably.

"How did you do that?"

"Simple energy to matter conversion."

"Huh?"

"I assume they have science and math where you're from." He spoke with an air of superiority. Daphne nibbled on her bottom lip and did her best to avoid rolling her eyes again. She tugged on the hem of her skirt to keep her hands busy. Without something to keep them busy, she was likely to smack that arrogant expression off his face.

"Of course, but what does that have to do with anything?"

"Knowledge of matter and energy are the building blocks to all magic." Daphne yawned. "I'm sorry princess, was I not using small enough words?"

"Excuse me for still being on a 24 hour day. We can't all have our lives disrupted and just go with the flow. So save the egotistical bull crap. I'm really not in the mood." Daphne took a deep breath and unclenched her hem. "I'm not stupid."

"I apologize. The fault was mine. I should have more sympathy. It's been so long I can't remember what it was like. You'll get used to the time difference. The moon phase schedule isn't standard across the tri-system. Just on the planet. I'm from one of the satellites. Up there we use a timing system that's something completely different." He opened a book and flipped the pages. "Why don't we start here?"

"That page is in English!" Daphne squealed like a school girl meeting her favorite popstar. She reached out eagerly and Marcus handed the book to her.

"My master's wife translated it for you. I think she's from your dimension. Probably not from the same reality though."

"Really? Was she dragged her by bounty hunters too?"

"I don't think so. She once said something about the Brumada Square."

"I think you mean Bermuda Triangle."

"Whatever. Why don't you read that and give it a try."

Daphne scanned the page. By the time she got to the end, she was shaking her head. It was instructions on gathering energy and making it visible.

"That's impossible. There's no way."

"It doesn't have to be a sphere. I'll settle for a spark."

"But—"

"Don't think about the logistics of it. Just do it. It's easier than you might think."

"Sure thing Yoda."

Daphne closed her eyes and tried to clear her mind. She couldn't completely ignore the inner voice telling her that this was a waste of time. She laughed inwardly. This reminded her of all the times she used to run around her house with a towel tied around her neck pretending to be a super hero. She opened her eyes and shook her head.

"I'm hopeless."

"I'd say so," Marcus said matter-of-factly.

"Gee, thanks for the encouragement."

"No one gets it on the first try."

"You did, if I recall," Steele chimed in.

"I'm an exception," Marcus said, mostly for Daphne's benefit. The compliment didn't stop him from holding his head higher and straightening his shoulders. The corners of his mouth twitched up and down as he fought back a smile. "Everyone can use their entire brain, but it takes training. Only a handful are born being able to do it right away. Not everyone is special."

"I know that," Daphne said, trying not to let her frustration show in her voice. Back home, she was at the top of her class. She'd never gotten less than an A- in her entire school career, and despite the insanity of what Marcus was asking her to do, she didn't want to fail.

"It's not about mentally being able to access that part of your mind," Marcus whispered. He put a reassuring hand on her knee. "It's a matter of relaxing and opening your spirit to the possibilities. Let go of your inhibitions and let it become instinct."

Daphne pushed his hand away. She closed her eyes and tried again. Still nothing. She frowned. "Isn't there some kind of magic aptitude test? Maybe I just stink at all this stuff."

"Actually, that's not a bad idea. I'll have master prepare one for you."

"I was kidding."

Marcus was already on his feet. "I'll be back tomorrow. In the meantime, study these." He handed her a stack of books, a tablet of blank paper and a pen.

"Please don't tell me this is the alphabet."

"The book on the top has the base letters and symbols. The others are your assignments and I think there's two reference."

"This thing has to be five inches thick. You can't expect me to learn all this in one day."

"Runey is pretty complex. If nothing else, it should keep you pretty busy. And also, you should work on these." He handed her a thin pamphlet written in English.

"What's this?"

"Meditations to help you control your body's cosmic and the cosmic around you."

"Right. Okay, maybe it's just me but do you have any idea how crazy you sound?" Marcus ignored her as he quickly packed the remaining books and papers into a leather messenger bag.

"I guess that's it for today. Oh, you were asking me about hidden pockets. Is that thing what you were trying to conceal?" Daphne nodded. "Do you mind if I have a look?"

She handed the device over. He turned the mp3 player in his hands. He tossed it in the air several times and bounced it gently in the palm of his hand.

"Stand up." Marcus sized her up with his eyes. He placed one hand on her shoulder and held the one with the mp3 player a few inches away from her waist. There was a sudden flash of pale orange light and the device was gone.

"Where did…what did you do?"

"It's in a hidden pocket."

"But I can't even feel the weight of it."

"That's why they're called hidden pockets."

"And how do I get it out of my pocket?"

He flashed an impish grin.

"When you figure it out, I'll teach you something else."

"But that's not fair."

"Consider it motivation for you to study."

"But—"

"You heard your teacher kid," Steele cut in. "Hit the books." He gestured toward the stairs.

"I don't believe this," she grumbled. "It's a conspiracy to make the next five years of my life a living hell." Daphne shifted the weight of the books around and carried them to her room. Steele waited until he heard her door slam before he addressed Marcus.

"Well, what do you think?"

"I'm just an apprentice, so my opinion doesn't count for much."

"It counts plenty or I wouldn't have asked."

"Honestly, I don't think you have anything to worry about."

"What makes you say that?"

"Because the real sorceress Katz wouldn't have fallen for the oldest trick in the book." He slipped a small metal rectangle from his pocket and tossed it to Steele. The hunter caught the object and laughed. He didn't have to look down to know it was Daphne's mp3 player.

"She could just be playing a part."

Marcus shook his head. "The Katz's don't like being made fools of. They pride themselves on always being two steps ahead of their enemies. Subtlety is not in their vocabulary."

"You speak as if you have personal experience."

"See you tomorrow."

CHAPTER 20

"So, what'd I miss?" Agent Johnston asked. The sound of flushing trailed behind him as he closed the bathroom door with his foot. He tucked his shirt in and quickly slipped on a black blazer. He checked the fit of the jacket in the hotel's mirror before splashing a little water on his hands.

"The father's still on the phone with the lawyer," Agent Isles said. "The mall is trying to sue the family due to the allegations of this being terrorism related."

"What about the brother?"

"Sutton and McGhee have been trailing him for hours. I think he knows he's being followed. This town isn't very big and they've had to stop for gas twice."

Johnston chuckled. "Cheeky devil. Tell them to keep on him. If he so much as pees in a bush I want to know about it."

"Yes sir."

"Where are Watson and Rodriguez?"

"Watson's getting a nap before his shift and Tony's at the local diner on a food run."

"I thought I told him to order in."

"This is rural America sir. They don't have delivery."

Johnston dried his hands on a thin towel. He slapped some water on his face and groaned as he patted his face dry. He sauntered over to the kitchenette and poured himself the last of the coffee. The coffee had been sitting there since this morning. He took a sip and fought the urge to gag. It was cold and gritty. The cheap grounds, coupled with a cheap filter made the liquid almost intolerable. He added cream and stirred it with a plastic spoon before nuking it in the microwave. He stirred it again and took another taste before joining Isles at the computer. He pulled a cheap rattan chair over to where the I.T. man was sitting. Isles leaned to the left, allowing his superior a good look over his shoulder.

"So, what am I looking at?" Johnston asked.

"The Morrow's entire house. There's the kitchen, the back yard, the garage, living room, the home office and the kid's room. There's only audio in the bathroom and the master." With each room he named, the screen shifted to a clear view of the space. He clicked back to the home office and gestured to the monitor on his right which showed a split screen view of every room in the house.

"What's she doing?"

"She's been on the computer all day."

"Doing what?"

"Research. She's looked into everything from UFO sightings, alien abductions, crop circles, presumed cover-ups. You name it, she's seen it."

"What about the cousin?"

"Galen's on his way back to Phoenix. We've got agents tailing him. Don't worry sir. Agents from the Phoneix branch have been through his place. Wire taps and surveillance equipment is already in place. We also did the girlfriend's place in case he thinks he can outsmart us and stay there. Danick is going over his financials as we speak and we should have his background check within the hour."

"It's been a month and we're just now finding out if he has a criminal record?"

"I apologize sir, but the parents were our first priority." Isles looked over his shoulder. Johnston was leaning back in his chair stirring his coffee. His unwashed black hair was hanging in his face and he gently stroked the dark stubble on his chin. He was staring at the floral curtain hanging above the air conditioner. The air conditioning unit hummed and clicked back on.

"Sir, may I have permission to ask a personal question?"

"What is it?"

"You don't really think what happened to these people's kid was really terrorists related, do you?" He adjusted his glasses and flexed his back before hunching back over the keyboard.

"Our job is to investigate and give an accurate report to our superiors. I don't get paid to speculate."

"Hmn. I see."

Johnston scratched his facial hair and watched Isles work for a few minutes. The light from the computer screen was reflected in the younger man's blue eyes. There was a tiny piece of lint in the other man's short blonde hair.

"Before I answer, tell me something. Do you really believe in little green men?"

"I'm a skeptic sir. At least, I was before this case. Now, and I hope you won't think less of me when I say this, but I really hope it was terrorists."

"Really? Why?"

"A man, I can fight. His weaknesses are no different than my own. But super intelligent life from another planet…we don't stand a chance."

"Like I said, I don't speculate. But if I was going to hazard a guess, not that I would, but if I did, I'd say I think that thing definitely wasn't from Earth. And that's why we have to keep an eye on this family. There's a reason that this thing chose them. I don't believe in coincidence. These people must have a connection with these beings. It could be genetic or it could be any number of things. Whatever it is they know something and it's our job to figure out what that something is. The fate of the human race may very well depend on it."

"Sir, then may I make a suggestion?"

"About?"

"Well, you know the old saying 'you catch more flies with honey than vinegar'."

Johnston smiled. He downed the rest of his coffee and set the cup on the floor. "I'm listening. What exactly do you have in mind?"

Addison Morrow parked her car beside the road. Her yard and driveway were blocked by U-Hauls and black SUVs. She slammed her car door and trudged through wet grass. The tip of her pantyhose peeking out from the front of her open toed shoes was soaked by the time she reached the front door. The cool fall air chilled her toes and made them feel almost numb. Addison pushed past agents who seemed oblivious to her prescence.

"Mrs. Morrow," a man in a dark suit approached her. He extended his hand to offer a hand shake. She folded her arms across her chest. He lowered his hand and wiped it nervously against his pant leg. "I'm Agent Johnston."

"We've met."

"I'm in charge of your family's case."

"I see. Emptying Daphne's room wasn't enough for you people? Is that it? Come to take everything else we own? While you're at it, why don't you just lock us away without a proper trial?"

"On the contrary, we're putting your daughter's things back. The agents should be done in less than an hour. When we're gone, you should find everything just as it was before. It will be as if we were never here."

"I don't believe this," Addison breathed. "So you no longer think we're terrorists?"

"No ma'am we don't. As far as I'm concerned you and your husband are the victims here. I sincerely apologize for any inconvenience our investigation may have caused. I know we didn't make this difficult time in your life easy, but I hope you understand we were just doing our jobs."

"Agent Johnston," Isles interrupted, "I'm sorry to interrupt but we've got a situation."

"Of course. Mrs. Morrow, if you'll excuse me."

"Wait." She grabbed his arm as he attempted to edge past her.

"Was there something else?"

"No. Yes. If we're no longer suspects then does that mean you know what happened to Daphne?"

"I understand that you're curious about your daughter's whereabouts." He paused as Addison nodded. One by one he pried her fingers from his wrist. "Ma'am that information is highly classified. I can't discuss it at this time. However, if you and your husband would be willing to meet with my team and I in private I'd be more than happy to tell you everything we know."

"How about this evening?"

"This evening?"

"Sir," Agent Isles urged.

"Yes agent. In a moment." He turned his attention back to Daphne's mother. "I'm sorry, but this evening's no good. We're following up on a few leads. We'll be available tomorrow evening if you can fit us into your schedule."

"Yes, of course. Is it alright if we do it here?"

"Yes, that would fine. Now, if you'll excuse me I really must be going." Addison let go of Johnston's sleeve. He exited through the front door. He leaned close to Isles and appeared to be whispering something. Addison stood watching as the remainder of Daphne's things were brought in. She reached to steady herself against the sofa. The room felt slanted and she sank against the soft cushions. She ran her fingers through her hair and grasped absentmindedly at her scalp. She didn't notice as the agents finished their work and left.

When Emory returned he found his wife crying into a pillow.

"Addie, what is it?" he asked as he dropped his briefcase onto the floor. He shrugged off his overcoat and draped it over the back of the sofa.

"The feds brought all her stuff back today."

"You're not serious. Have you been up there? Have you seen it?"

She shook her head. "I've been too afraid to see. They promised that it looks just like it did before."

"Well did they say what happened to her? Do they know anything?"

"We're supposed to meet with an Agent Johnston tomorrow. He said he'll tell us everything. I just hope to God that—."

"Shh! Don't say it." Emory wrapped his arms around her and held her close. He buried his face in her hair and breathed in the fading scent of apple body wash. "Please, don't say it."

CHAPTER 21

"Well, this is a rare treat. If I didn't know any better, I'd say you were actually looking forward to my daily visit." Marcus said playfully. He smiled broadly as he wiped his feet on the synthetic straw mat.

Daphne rolled her eyes and held the door open for him. "Wow. I thought you were putting on a show the first time we met. But now that I know you, I see you really must be a morning person."

"No. No I'm not. I actually despise getting up early, but the weekly paycheck helps."

Daphne chuckled and shook her head. "You're terrible. So are you coming in or not?" She took a step back to give him more room to cross the threshold.

"How about you? You're up before the sun without prompting. I'd say that early rising is starting to agree with you."

"Not likely." Daphne slammed the front door and secured the chain latch. "Sit down and let's get this over with." She gestured to her workbook, which was lying open on the coffee table.

"Ah and there it is, that charming morning demeanor I've come to know and love," Marcus said sarcastically.

"It's not my morning demeanor that's the problem. It's you people and your obvious aversion to sunlight."

Marcus laughed and settled on the couch. He pulled the book close enough to allow him to lean over and scan the pages. He whipped out a pen and made a few corrections before flipping to the next page. With each page the dark blue marks he made grew in number. He took a break to flex his fingers. Out of the corner of his eye his gaze followed Daphne like a cat stalking its prey before he exploded.

"For the cosmos' sake, would you stop pacing around like some caged animal and just have a seat? I can't concentrate."

"Sorry." Daphne mumbled as she flopped onto the far end of the sofa. She let out a sigh and rested her chin in her right hand. She proceeded to twirl a strand of curly brown hair around her left index finger. She ground her teeth and muttered quietly to herself.

"Is there something bothering you?"

"No. Just grade it. Put me out of my misery."

"Is this what's bothering you? You should try to relax. You take yourself too seriously."

"You just don't get it."

"Runey is a difficult language. Give yourself some time. You've only been learning for a few weeks."

"That's easy to say when you're some kind of genius."

"I'm no genius."

"Yeah, well that's not how Steele tells it. He's constantly praising your skill and abilities and telling me how lucky I am to have you as a teacher."

"So, you're jealous?"

"Hardly."

He turned to another page and made a face. Should I even bother to check the rest of this, he thought.

"Back home I was at the top of my class. I was hoping to go to college a year early, not reading 'A is for Apple'."

"Wow. You need more help than I thought. The book I gave you was 'S is for Salamander'."

"I'm not in the mood for your jokes Marcus. And I was being sarcastic." She growled out a sigh. "I guess I'm just not used to this feeling."

"What feeling?"

"Humility."

"Okay." He closed the workbook and set the pen on top of it. "That's it. You and I are going out."

"Excuse me?"

"It's obvious you've been in this house too long. A little fresh air will do you good."

"Thanks for the offer, but I'm not allowed. Steele's orders."

"You're joking."

"Nope. I haven't been past the front porch since I went shopping with Kember."

"That's exactly my point. I think your studies would benefit from a little real world experience."

"But I'm not supposed to go outside without permission. And let's face it Steele still thinks I'm Diamara Katz in disguise. He'd never allow it."

"Well where's Steele? I'll ask him for you."

"He's not here."

"Kember then?"

Daphne shook her head. "I haven't seen either of them for days. Steele said he had a job and Kember kind of flits in and out as she pleases."

"So you're all alone here."

"Try not to look so worried. I can take care of myself. Sure I'm almost out of food, but I'm like a hamster. I can survive on just water and shreds of lettuce for weeks. What?"

"I was just thinking that if I were worried you were an evil sorceress, I wouldn't leave you alone and give you the opportunity to escape."

"Come on. You don't really think he's working?" she said, making air quotes to emphasis the last word. "He's probably hiding in the woods watching me, just waiting for me to poke my head outside that door so he can—"

"You've got some imagination kid." Steele cut in.

Both Daphne and Marcus jumped. She felt a sharp pain in her neck as she twitched her neck in his direction. Steele sauntered down the stairs and paused on his way to the kitchen. "I wouldn't waste that much time and effort on someone who can't even gather light energy."

"Where did you come from?" Marcus asked.

"Back entrance."

"There's a back entrance?" Daphne asked. "Wait. Better question, where have you been? I thought you were working?"

He shrugged. "And leave you here to plot your escape? I don't think so."

"We weren't plotting." Marcus argued. "I was just making a suggestion."

"And I told him it was a bad idea."

"Why would you say that? I think it should be fine."

"What?"

"You can go out if you want to."

"But you said I couldn't go outside."

"I said you couldn't go outside without permission. And you have my permission as long as Marcus goes with you."

"And I need a babysitter because?"

"Arret is a dangerous place. It's nothing like your world. And it's especially dangerous for someone with your features."

"What do you mean? Because I look like her?"

He turned his back and headed into the kitchen. "Shouldn't you two be going? The sun'll be up soon."

"Well, you heard him." Marcus was on his feet and already undoing the latch. "Let's not give him a chance to change his mind."

Daphne followed her tutor onto the porch. Marcus closed the door behind her and skipped down the front steps. She was greeted by the chirping of birds and bugs. Thick dark woods surrounded the little house like a security fence. She took a deep breath and breathed in the warm morning air. The dark sky was dotted with billions of stars. Only a quarter of one of the two moons was visible this morning. She breathed out and took the porch steps one at a time.

"So, where exactly are we going?"

"You'll see."

"Where's your car?"

"Apprentices can't afford cars. They have to walk."

"Is it a long walk?"

"You'll see."

Daphne groaned. "First I have to get up early and now I have to exercise. Do you and Steele get together and think up ways to make my life more miserable?"

He smiled, took her hand and gently tugged her forward. "Come on, it's really not that far."

Marcus led her down one barely visible footpath after another. The sun had already risen before she realized the house and the forest had faded from view. The mostly flat terrain laden with rocks and hidden tree roots had become grassy hills. Daphne was relieved to leave behind the hard ground and exchange it for rolling meadows carpeted with wild flowers. Each step sent a crowd of butterflies fluttering into the air.

"Here's as good a place as any." Marcus pulled a star patterned blanket from his messenger bag. He spread it on the ground and gestured for Daphne to have a seat. "You're wearing pants today so I hope you don't mind if we take a break."

"I don't need to rest."

"You look like you're about to pass out."

"I'm fine."

"Don't be silly. Your face is all red. Plus the way you were huffing and puffing up those last few hills, I'm surprised you made it this far. I really thought I was going to have to carry you."

"I warn you, if I sit down, I may never get up again." Daphne sank onto the blanket. Her muscles were burning and she struggled to catch her breath. Marcus produced two sandwiches and two bottles of flavored water. He offered half the food to Daphne and took his sandwich and lay on his back. He took a bite and watched the clouds drift by overhead.

"You're gonna choke if you eat like that," she said between bites. Marcus ignored her and took a larger bite. He chewed slowly with exaggerated motions of his jaw. Daphne rolled her eyes.

"Fine, suit yourself, but if you start choking I'm just gonna sit here and watch."

Marcus sat up and took a long drink from his bottle of water. He cleared his throat, opened his mouth and then closed it again. He took another sip of water. "You…you're—"

"I'm sick. Yeah I know. So are you gonna tell me where we're going?"

"Wizards Portal."

"Wizards Portal? Is that a wormhole type portal?" Daphne asked hopefully.

"Before you get your hopes up I should warn you, it's just the name for the gateway where I live."

"Oh. So a gateway's like a neighborhood?"

"A what?"

"Never mind."

"By the way, you look nice today. Is that new?"

"Thank you and yes. Madam Pietryson delivered the rest of my stuff yesterday. It feels good to finally be out of that dress."

"I can imagine. Not that the dress didn't suit you. It did, but after seeing it every day, I was beginning to feel sorry for you."

"You should feel sorry for me every second."

"Oh? How did you come to that conclusion?"

"With a master like Steele, I think I deserve all the sympathy I can get. I swear he gets his kicks thinking up ways to make me miserable."

"You need to lighten up. That's just one of the perks of being a master. What's the point of having an apprentice if you can't have a little fun every once in a while?"

"Then I take it your master enjoys practical jokes at your expense as well?"

"No. Master Hilia doesn't have a sense a humor. He's a class 12 wizard. He doesn't have time for anything but creating more work for me to do. He's a real slave driver. To tell you the truth, I'd kill for one day with a master as laid back as Steele."

"Steele? Laid back?"

"Believe it or not, he goes easy on you. He lets you get away with a lot."

"Oh. So, this place we're going to, are there a lot of your kind there? You know wizards?"

"I'm still an apprentice. I'm only in my second year."

"Okay. Apprentice. What does a wizard do?"

"We study magic. We work on expanding magical knowledge, creating new spells and ways of blending magic and technology."

"Is it possible to make a living doing research?"

"Most of our magic-tech crosses are done on commission and we get a royalty for every piece sold. We also print and sell The Codex. It's published yearly and includes an updated collection of books on magic history, spells, counter spells; that sort of thing."

"Like an encyclopedia. I see. So, is your guild the only one that prints a codex?"

"I don't think so. As far as I know every guild prints one, but my master and his associates only deal in complex magic and magic theory. So our clientele is pretty exclusive. Our neighbor deals in study tools though. He sells me your books at a discount."

"Does Hyron reimburse you for that sort of thing?"

"If I say no would that make you study harder?"

"Ha!" Daphne laughed and gave him a playful shove. "I'm already giving you 110%. If I tried any harder I think my head would explode."

"Are you going to finish that?" Marcus asked. Daphne handed him the uneaten half of her sandwich and he wolfed it down. She offered him her water. "No thanks. You really should drink the rest of that. Trust me. You'll thank me later." He checked the time on a pocket watch and leaned back, supporting himself on his elbows. He stretched his legs out and crossed them at the ankles.

As she sipped slowly on the sweet liquid, Daphne cast her eyes upward. She coughed and sputtered as peach flavored water flowed into her lungs and some went up her nose. Marcus sat up quickly and patted her firmly on her back until the coughing ceased and she was breathing normally.

"Are you alright?"

"Yeah," Daphne croaked. Her eyes were still pinned on the sky.

Marucs glanced up and then back at look of shock frozen on Daphne's face. "What's the matter?"

"The clouds. They're light purple."

"Yeah. So?"

"Where I come from, clouds are white."

"Is that all?"

"I can't believe I never noticed it before."

"If you're fine we should get going." Daphne crawled off the blanket and struggled to stand. Marcus helped her to her feet before shaking out the fabric. Bread crumbs and flower petals flew into the air. He carefully folded the blanket and tucked it back in his bag.

"Marcus, can I ask you a question?"

"Sure."

"How is it that we can speak the same language but you read in another?"

"Well that has to do with something that happened around the beginning of recorded history." He stored the empty bottles and gestured for her to follow. He took the pace much slower this time. "The first magicians were a small group of people who formed a secret society. They used magic to rule over the weak. As time passed, they began to worry that the people might learn magic and turn on them. They developed Runey as a code to help them keep the knowledge to themselves."

"Wow."

"These women and their descendants ruled for generations until the secret was eventually discovered. The people rebelled and after centuries of tyranny and a long, bloody war, the magicians were defeated. Since magic had been such a large part of society for so long, the Runey language just sort of stuck."

"Well, if it took centuries for the rest of the world to learn it, I guess I shouldn't feel so bad."

"Actually, I'm kind of surprised that Runey and magic doesn't come easier to you."

"Why would you be surprised? Magic doesn't exist on my planet."

"It's just…well the first magicians were actually sorceresses. They were all members of the Katz family."

"But I'm not a Katz." Daphne spat.

"Technically, you are. Even though you're from a different dimension, your DNA is virtually descended from theirs."

Daphne sighed. "I suppose there's no point in arguing with you. People see what they want to see."

"When you really think about it, it makes sense with what Steele said."

"What? You mean that comment about my face? I'm aware I look like her. There's no point in reminding me."

"Sorry it's not that. I was just remembering something I learned in history class." He turned to Daphne and locked eyes with her. "I don't think Steele was talking about your face."

"He said the world is dangerous for someone with features like mine. I don't understand what else he could have meant."

"He was referring to your eyes."

"My eyes? What about my eyes? What's wrong with them?"

"Nothing. Just the color."

"Don't people have different color eyes on this planet?"

"Yes, but green is a very rare color on this world. Unfortunately for you, it's a very obvious color."

"Define obvious."

"Only members of the Katz family have green eyes. It marks them as some of the most powerful sorcerers. As far as the people are concerned that makes you a member of the most hated and most dangerous crime family in the tri-system."

"But I'm not—"

"I know that and Steele knows that, but it won't matter to anyone else. No one will ever take the time to get to know you. They only care about what they can see."

She clenched her jaw and nibbled her lip as she blinked back angry tears.

"I'm sorry. I just thought I should tell you."

"Well I really wish you hadn't. I suppose it was stupid of me to think the next five years wouldn't completely suck."

"Daphne—"

"Don't bother. I don't want to hear it."

"I'm sorry. I just thought it would be better if you weren't walking around oblivious."

"I guess you never heard of ignorance is bliss."

CHAPTER 22

"We're here." Marcus said, stopping in a valley between four large hills.

"It's just another meadow." Daphne stated. She looked around. The hills rose up at all the cardinal directions. They looked like mini mountains with peaks that seemed to kiss the sky. The wild flowers here grew so thick Daphne could barely move her legs. She knelt to caress the petals of a periwinkle colored flower.

"Please don't pick those." Marcus snapped.

He grabbed her arm and hauled her to her feet. As she rose, Daphne noticed that some of the flowers seemed to grow in a specific pattern. The periwinkle blossoms lay like a round carpet beneath them. Six lines of blue flowers about a foot wide spread away from the circle like the spokes of a wheel. The blue flowers seemed to climb up the sides of the hills and stop just short of the peaks. Each section of flowers was connected to another by a foot wide strip.

"It makes a circle," Daphne murmured.

The rest of the flowers filling in the gaps were a variety of colors. At first glance, they seemed to be growing randomly. Then they started glowing. Daphne gasped and took a step back. Orange and yellow petals lit up on her left forming the shape of a dragon.

To her right was a purple crane. Behind her was a red Pegasus and around her were several other shapes she couldn't recognize.

"Marcus!" She called her tutor's name, but the wind whipped by her. It felt as though the oxygen were ripped from her chest.

The wind continued to pick up speed, swirling around them in a cyclone while the flowers seemed unaffected. Marcus wrapped an arm around her waist and pulled her close to him. He pressed his lips close to her ear. She could feel the warmth of his breath but the wind stole all sound. The glowing images were swept into the cyclone. Their light grew and blended together until it blotted out her view of the flowers in the meadow.

Daphne's stomach lurched. The wind was suddenly knocked out of her. Her knees buckled. She was seeing spots. She was falling! She frantically wrapped her arms around Marcus's waist for support. She hadn't moved, yet she felt as if she were stumbling through a spinning tunnel in a funhouse.

Daphne sank onto the cool marble floor. Her body trembled and she gasped for air. Her stomach was still doing summersaults. She was glad she hadn't eaten the whole sandwich or she would have lost her lunch. Her arms had slid downward and were now loosely draped around Marcus's ankles.

"You okay?" She nodded as he lifted her off the floor. He let her lean against him. "I guess multi-phasics doesn't agree with everyone." Daphne did her best to glare at him. Marcus suppressed a laugh. In this state, her stare didn't have the same effect. She looked more like a drowned rat.

"I really hate you right now," she muttered pitifully.

"Duly noted," he said with a sarcastic smile. "Welcome to Wizards Portal." He swept his free arm outward in a game show model like gesture.

"Am I supposed to be impressed?" Daphne snapped, pushing him away. She stumbled a little as she struggled to regain her balance. Her color was starting to come back.

They were standing in a round foyer. The marble floor was patterned the same way as the flowers in the meadow. Only here the pictures were clearly defined. Instead of six blue paths, the blue spokes fanned out into 36 different directions. Each path stretched about six feet and continued beneath an archway. Light streamed in from above as if they were under stained glass. Daphne looked up and her eyes widened. There were no windows.

"You live here?" she asked.

"It gets better. Follow me." He looked as if he were going to take the most eastwardly path then veered slightly to the north at the last moment. "Are you coming in or not?" he asked, mimicking her tone from earlier in the day.

They entered the arch and he pushed open a door painted with a purple crane. She followed closely behind him. She took in a short audible breath as she took in the scene. The door clicked softly closed behind her. They were standing on cobblestone road just outside a small city.

The town looked like a collection of the cottages she'd imagined when her parents used to read 'Hansel and Gretl'. The buildings were made of stone. Some had straw roofs while others sported thick wooden shingles. The thick wooden doors didn't have locks and there were no bars on the windows. Instead, a collection of magic circles had been painted where the door and frame met. The same was true for the windows.

Each door was painted and decorated according to the homeowner's personal tastes. Some homes had flower or vegetable gardens out front and others had stone patios. Smoke rose in thin wisps from almost every chimney. The town was alive with the sounds of people working and chatting. The tinkle of wind chimes floated on the gentle breeze.

"Wow. It looks like something out of a fairy tale." Marcus smiled. He readjusted his bag strap and started walking. Daphne kept pace beside him. He walked slowly to allow her time to take in the view.

"It really is amazing," she breathed.

"I take it you're impressed?"

"It's beyond words. How did they make something like this? What keeps it all together?"

"We're contained in a natural pocket between planes."

"Try speaking my language for a change."

"There's the physical plane where we're from and where we typically exist and there's the ephemeral plane where creatures like Kember are from. And then there's the space in the middle where time still flows at the same pace and most of the laws of science and magic are the same. That middle area is sort of like a rock with occasional pockets of empty space."

"Uh huh. You know this is all just a little bit over my head."

He laughed nervously as they neared the town square. "Here," he handed her a pair of sunglasses. "You might want to put these on."

"I take it the Wizards Portal is a Katz free zone?" she grumbled bitterly.

"The elders already know you're coming. I had to get permission first, but it'll just cause less trouble if you go along with it."

"It's fine. You don't have to explain." Daphne made a point to reign in her sarcasm. The mysterious lighting in the place was starting to give her a headache and she was glad to have something to help block out some of the light. She just wasn't thrilled about having to hide her favorite feature as if she were a leper.

With each step Daphne's ability to keep pace faltered. She was already three feet behind Marcus when he chanced a glance over his shoulder. He waited for her to catch up as she shuffled her feet over the uneven stones.

"Hurry up. It's almost time for the afternoon meal. If I'm late, the master lets his little monsters eat my share."

"I'm going as fast as I can." Daphne grumbled. As she forced her legs to move faster, she gently massaged her temples. "I don't see how you can stand living in this place. Doesn't the light bother you?"

"No. But I've heard it takes some getting used to." He shrugged his shoulders and let the weight of the messenger bag shift slightly. "It's just down this street." He walked to the middle of the block and rang the bell on the door of a yellow stone house. The door swung open. Standing in the doorway was a woman of medium height with brown eyes and graying strawberry blonde hair swept into a bun.

"You're late," she said, crossing her arms across her chest and holding the door open with the toe of her right foot.

"I apologize my lady. Our guest was having a little trouble keeping up."

"What guest?"

Marcus looked behind him. Daphne was gone. "She was right-"

"Is that her?" the woman asked, gesturing with her head to a staggering figure three houses down.

"Daphne!" Marcus raced toward her, but it was too late. Her body was already careening sideways. Her forehead bounced against the curb and her body rolled into the edge of the street.

"It's my fault," Marcus said. He was on his knees before Masters Hilia and Steele. He had his head bowed at Hilia's feet. "She was complaining about headaches and I didn't register it until it was too late."

"Oh would you stop torturing the poor boy and let him up already?" Amber snapped at her husband. She brushed a stray strand of grayish red hair back into place. "It's only a bruise. She's lucky she has all that curly hair. It's what broke her fall."

Hilia looked at Steele. "I'll leave it to you then. She is your apprentice after all."

Steele rolled his eyes. "Get up Marcus. If Amber says she'll be fine then I really don't see a need for punishment. Go eat your dinner. It's probably cold by now."

"He'll be lucky if it's still there," Amber said. "He's been groveling so long the children have probably already divided it between them."

Daphne moaned. "Ow." She gently touched her hand to her forehead. She winced. She could feel a bandage. "Really Steele? You're just going to let him off the hook? I thought he was supposed to be looking after me."

"Don't start. This was your idea."

"When did I ever say I wanted to walk a thousand miles and be transmorphed into the center of the earth?"

"See," he said to Hilia, "now I know there's nothing wrong with her. I'd only be worried if she didn't have an attitude."

"I can hear you." Daphne snapped.

Steele turned to Daphne. "As I recall, you were the one who asked for a magic aptitude test."

"Exactly what part of today was a test?"

"Only someone with an extremely high magic aptitude can enter Wizards Portal without the assistance of technology, let alone survive it for any length of time," Hilia explained.

"And this is important because?" Daphne asked.

"It means the reason your skills aren't progressing is because you're lazy," he finished matter-of-factly.

"Lazy? I'm not lazy. I've never had a teacher call me lazy in all my life. Argh!" She cradled her hands around her forehead. "How do you people stand it here? Gosh, I feel like my head is going to explode."

"It's one of the side effects of Wizards Portal," Amber explained. "It's a safeguard put in place to help you learn control and restraint."

"At least it's not deliberate. I was beginning to think it was a direct attack because of who my double is."

"Oh," Amber said, "we took down most of the DNA safeguards just before you came through the main gate. That overwhelming feeling of nausea was just a small taste of the poison we laced the portal with. If you hadn't been with Marcus, it probably would've killed you."

"Probably? How do you know it wouldn't have?"

She handed Daphne a small bottle. "Look familiar?" It was a bottle of the peach water Marcus had given her when they stopped to rest.

"I don't believe this. You people are seriously trying to kill me."

"Think of it as a warning," Hilia said. "You may not have committed any sins on this world, but if you do, no force in all the cosmos will be able to stop us from putting an end to you. We've had centuries of practice."

"Am I supposed to quiver with fear?"

"She certainly is feisty," Hilia said to Steele. "Perfect hunter material." The wizard draped his arm around the mercenary's neck and they left the room together.

Daphne rolled her eyes. "And they said he doesn't have a sense of humor." She sighed. "This is going to be a long five years," she groaned. Amber laughed. She poured some peach water into a cup and added a blue powder from a small bowl. She stirred it with a wooden spoon and offered the cup to Daphne. "And what's this?"

"It'll help ease the pain. You're staying here tonight and you'll never get any sleep with those headaches. Trust me, I know."

Daphne took the cup but she didn't take a sip. "How do I know I can trust you?" she asked. The woman poured herself a cup and added some of the same blue powder to hers. She downed the cup in three swallows.

"Satisfied?"

Daphne shrugged. "You can never be too careful. I am on a planet where it seems everybody wants me dead." She sipped slowly at the water and felt the pain in her head slowly began to ease.

CHAPTER 23

Daphne rubbed sleep from her eyes as she followed the smell of fresh squeezed juice and cinnamon rolls. She pushed open the swinging door and entered the kitchen. The walls were painted a bright yellow and pictures of cardinals and blue jays had been stenciled along the center of the wall like a chair rail. There were three children sitting at the table stuffing food into their mouths as if they hadn't seen a meal in days. With their cheeks stuffed full they looked like three red headed chipmunks. Marcus was leaning against the kitchen counter with a mug of coffee in his hands. Amber was putting glaze on a plate of cinnamon rolls.

"Good morning slacker," he teased.

"Yeah whatever, shut-up." Daphne snapped.

Amber slid the plate of rolls across the counter to her. "I saved some for you. Consider it my official welcome to Wizards Portal."

"Mmm. Perfect. Tastes just like Pillsbury," Daphne said. She closed her eyes and savored the taste of warm cinnamon roll. She licked the glaze off her fingers and slowly ate another one.

"I don't know about that. I've had a lot of time to practice, but I still think something's missing."

"Tastes like home," Daphne said softly. She opened her eyes and ran her slightly sticky fingers through her curly hair.

"Amber?"

"Hmn?"

"Can I ask you a question?"

"Sure, go ahead."

"Yesterday, the wizard master said that I wouldn't have made it past the gate if I wasn't powerful enough."

"That's right."

"Then what happens to people who aren't powerful enough?"

"Nothing happens. The portal simply doesn't open. It's a safeguard that was installed during the revolution to keep the rebel base a secret. Without special technology, no one can achieve a trans-phasic state unless they have the magical ability to do it on their own. Once inside Wizards Portal, there's machinery in place to help you stay phased."

"Oh."

"I know that face," Marcus said, setting his cup on the counter.

"What face? I'm not making a face."

"Go on, just say it."

"Well I wasn't making a face. I was just wondering if what the wizard guy said was true. Maybe he was pulling my leg." The statement was greeted with blank stares. "You know, joking."

"Master Hilia doesn't have a sense of humor," Marcus and Amber said in unison.

"Then he really does think I'm lazy."

"Believe me, I know how hard you're trying Daphne," Marcus said. "I don't think you're lazy."

"Then why can't I do it? I'm trying as hard as I can. But no matter what I do, I'm still a failure."

"Maybe you're trying too hard," Amber offered.

"You really think that's her problem?" Marcus asked. Daphne narrowed her eyes at him.

"Look I don't know if we're from the same Earth or not, but I've been on this world a long time. One thing I've learned is that over thinking the magic thing can really get in the way. And the other thing I've learned, is that what slows down people like you and me is how closed off we are from the reality around us."

"I'm not closed off. I'm here. I'm doing my homework and I study all the time."

"It's not enough. You have to want it. You don't have to be the best, but you should at least learn enough to survive."

"What if I never figure it out?"

"Then you're screwed." She looked at Daphne's shocked face and shrugged. "Oh Marcus, I have a few errands I need you to run today."

"Of course. I'll take care of it as soon as I take Daphne home."

"Take her with you," Steele said, entering the kitchen. He poured himself a cup of coffee and squeezed in next to the children. "I have some business and I'm going out of town for a few days."

He tossed Daphne a solitary key. She barely caught it before it hit the floor. It was attached to small pink rectangle. It was see through. The inside looked like the interior of a tiny computer.

"What's this for?"

"The front door."

Marcus let out a whistle. "Wow. A fuschia level merc card."

"Don't get too excited. It's prepaid. I did some reading. Seems hamsters need something other than lettuce and water."

"So you were spying on me."

"Make sure she gets a good deal. That money's got to last until I get back."

"And just how long do you plan on being gone?"

"Like I'd tell you."

"Well is Kember coming back then?"

He shrugged. "Don't know? She tends to do as she pleases." Amber set a plate on the table in front of him. She passed him a fork and shooed her kids away from the table.

"Ugh." Daphne groaned. She crossed her arms and rolled her eyes.

"I'm surprised those things haven't rolled out of your head," he snapped.

"You sound like my mother."

Steele shot her a mean look before he shoved a fork full of scrambled eggs in his mouth. "Just stay out of trouble."

Amber handed Marcus a list and gently pushed him toward the door. "Be back by second moon rise or Hilia will have your head."

"Yes ma'am." Marcus bowed respectfully to Amber.

Daphne followed closely behind Marcus as he wove his way through the crowded streets. They'd exited Wizards Portal and made a two hour walk to the nearest town. She reached up and adjusted the sunglasses. It felt strange to be wearing glasses again, especially ones that hadn't been fitted for her face.

Thinking about glasses made Daphne think about Dr. Ouji. While her time on the Templar prison transport had been terrifying and miserable, she couldn't help but smile at the memory of the kindly doctor. He'd fed her, kept her company and given her a reason to hope that things would turn out in her favor.

"What are you smiling about?" Marcus asked.

She shook her head. "Nothing. So," she asked, "where are we supposed to go first?"

"I think we should get something to eat."

"Is it time for lunch already?"

"We've been walking all morning. And since you're out, you might as well get a real look at Arret culture."

"Do you realize your planet's name is just terra spelled backwards?"

Marcus counted the letters on his fingers and mouthed to two words. "So?"

"Terra means Earth."

"Uh huh. Are you hungry or not?"

"Well when I think about it, I guess so."

"Good, then let's eat."

"I don't know if I should. I don't even know how much money is on this thing," she said, gesturing to the pocket with the key and the merc card.

"Don't worry, it's on me. Just stay close. I know a great little out of the way place."

The restaurant was one of those hole-in-the-walls that only locals know about. From the outside it looked like a condemned building. Marcus held open a door that appeared to be falling off its hinges. He placed his hand on the small of Daphne's back and guided her inside.

The heels of her new boots clicked over the newly refinished hardwood floors. Strings of white butterfly shaped lights had been hung from the center of the ceiling and spiraled out in all directions, forming a giant makeshift chandelier. Each small square table was dressed with a turquoise tablecloth. Silver plates and flatware had been laid out at every place. White cloth napkins had been folded into the shape of bow ties and placed in the center of each salad plate.

There was a stage against the far wall. A band was playing soft classical style music. The maître d showed them to a table near the stage. Daphne pushed the sunglasses up her nose and allowed the headwaiter to pull her chair out for her. She slipped as gracefully as she could into the seat and he pushed her chair in before handing her a menu. He waited until Marcus was seated before bowing politely and returning to his post.

Daphne opened the menu and scanned the Runey symbols. She could only read a few words. She closed the menu and looked around. The style of dress was more flamboyant than anything she'd seen so far. Almost everyone wore a cape or hooded cloak. She was surrounded by a sea of spandex and velvet.

"It looks like a convention for Vegas magicians. I've never seen so many capes and sequins in my life."

"Marcus, is that you?" a female voice called.

Daphne looked over her shoulder. A girl with short black hair cut asymmetrically bounced toward them. Her hair was streaked with dark purple. She was wearing blackish purple mascara dusted with glitter and purple glitter lipstick. Her black spandex body suit had been bedazzled with tiny crystals. She wore a purple shrug covered in pink sparkles and her left ear had been pierced eight times. The top seven earrings were simple gold hoops while the bottom earring was a diamond stud with long gold tassels hanging from it. Hanging from her neck was a pink crystal rabbit wearing a purple top hat.

The girl pulled up a chair from another table, turned it backwards and straddled it. She looked Daphne up and down. She wrinkled her nose, rolled her blue eyes, and turned her attention to the young wizard. She propped her elbows on the table and cradled her chin on her knuckles. On each of her ring fingers was a solid pink crystal band. The rings caught the white light from above and cast a soft glow on the girl's youthful alabaster skin.

"Did Hilia finally let you out of your cage?"

"Veda, what are you doing here? I thought Master Ember didn't approve of frivolity."

"Didn't you hear? I graduated two months early. I'm a full-fledged member of Top Hats and Rabbits."

"Congratulations. I'm so proud of you. And I'll bet your mother is too."

"I don't know. She keeps hinting that she wants me to pay for a transfer to Mystic."

"Mystic huh?"

"Yes. They have prestige and they always get the best commissions, but I hear they treat apprentices and new graduates like slurg worms."

"I've heard similar tales to that affect."

"So, who's your friend?" she asked, turning to look at Daphne. She batted her eyelashes and flashed a fake smile, showing off her perfect teeth.

"This is Daphne. Her master and mine are friends."

"Daphne you say? What an unusual name. I thought I knew all the wizards and their apprentices."

He leaned forward and beckoned her close. "Well, she's not exactly a wizard's apprentice."

"She's right here, she can hear you, and she has a name," Daphne snapped.

Veda took Marcus' menu and opened it to the first page. "If you're not a wizard's apprentice, then what are you?"

"I'm—"

"Shh!" Marcus hissed.

"What are you so nervous about?" Veda asked. "It's not like this is a wizards only club. Who cares if you bring in a, whatever she is?"

"Hunter." Daphne growled through gritted teeth. "I'm a hunter's apprentice."

"Really?" Veda's eyebrows went up. "You don't seem like the type. Too mousy and scrawny, but to each their own I guess." She closed the menu and handed it back to Marcus.

"Well, I need to put my order in and get going. I've got my first show tonight."

"Really? Where?"

"I'm contracted to do a wedding for the eighth house of Valeri."

"Wow."

"I know. The royal family is hard to impress, but I hear they tip big."

"They've got you doing dinner shows? I thought your concentration was in advanced magic theory."

"It was, but you can't walk right into Codex production and archiving. You have to work your way up. Of course, it helps if you rub elbows with the right people." She spun the chair around and shoved it back under the table it came from. "Well, enjoy your lunch." She whipped out a pen and scrawled something on the palm of his hand. "Give me a call when you're not busy. I'd love for you to see my new place."

The alley didn't look that much different from one on Earth. A few pieces of trash littered the alley and stray animals that resembled cats and raccoons scavenged around in open garbage cans. There was barely enough room for two cars to pass by at the same time. The dumpster beside her looked clean enough to eat off. The stainless steel shone in the ephemeral glow of the street lamps and it didn't give off the rancid odor of rotting garbage.

Daphne pushed the sunglasses up on her head and used them as a headband to hold back her curly hair. Marcus had left her out here while he stepped inside a wizards only business. "I'll only be a minute," he'd said. Of course, he'd made that promise at around 20:00 hours. The sun had set and second moon rise had come and gone. Two half-moons hung in the sky and the stars were starting to come out. Daphne sighed and stuck her hands in her pockets. She leaned against the wall and kicked at some loose stones on the street.

"Excuse me." Daphne felt a soft tug on her sleeve. "Lady, do you know what time it is?" Daphne looked down. There was a towheaded boy gazing up at her.

"Sorry honey, I don't have a watch." The child blinked several times before he finally turned and ran away. "You're welcome!" Daphne called after him. "Brat."

A few minutes later Marcus emerged. Daphne had her back to him. He shook his head and pushed the sunglasses down. She shrieked, startled.

"You scared me!" she wheeled around and swatted at him with her left hand. She missed.

"I thought I told you to keep those on."

"It's too dark? How am I supposed to see perverts sneaking up on me?"

"Mmn hmn."

"Besides, nobody saw me."

"I guess it's alright. This area doesn't get much traffic. Just keep them on until we get back to Steele's."

"There she is," a familiar voice shouted. "See, I told you so."

The little boy had returned. This time he had three older boys with him. The boys were dressed in the flamboyant style of wizards. Daphne tipped the sunglasses up in order to get a good look at them. They were each dressed in orange and brown Kung Fu style suits. They too were no strangers to glitter and crystals. A dragon was embroidered on the one in the center. The body of the dragon covered the entire front of his shirt. Down each pant leg was the image of a dragon leg.

"I've known it all along," the one in the middle said. His forehead wrinkled as he took a step forward.

"You're mistaken Dauro." Marcus said calmly.

"Marcus, you filthy traitor. How dare you consort with the likes of them." The little one took a step back while the others advanced. The other two spread out and moved around as if to try and flank them. Marcus rolled up his sleeves. He dropped into a ready stance. His hands were an equal distance apart; his fingers curved like tiger paws. He lined up his feet and bent his knees.

"Think about what you're doing. If you just listen—" he tried to reason, but Dauro interrupted. His voice dripped disgust.

"When we're done with you, you'll wish you were dead," he said, his eyes beginning to glow orange.

"Daphne, you should run."

She took two steps backward before turning and taking off as fast as her legs could go. Behind her explosions rang through the night air. She took the first turn she came across and made sure to take as many as she could: first right, then left, left again and right. She threw a glance over her shoulder. She caught a glimpse of orange and brown glitter as she made another left.

"God, I really hope I'm not going in circles," she gasped.

The sound of the fighting grew faint. She made another left and bumped into two women with bulging fabric grocery bags. Some fruit spilled onto the ground. The sunglasses clattered to the ground.

"Sorry."

"Oh it's alright. Just be more careful…" Daphne reached down and retrieved a blue, lemon shaped object. She quickly held it out to the woman. The startled expression on the lady's faced changed to one of confusion and then boiled over into rage. She dropped her bag and let out a scream. Her eyes and hands began to glow. Daphne let the fruit fall to the ground and quickly dodged around her. She zigzagged out of the path of a fireball and took an immediate right.

"Don't let her get away!" one of the boys shouted.

She made a few more twists and turns. Daphne looked over her shoulder again. She'd lost one of them, but the other was still hot on her trail. Her lungs were burning. Her chest felt as if it were about to explode. Gasping, she slid around a corner just as lightning struck the wall of a building. The force of the explosion rocked loose some shingles sending clay plates raining down. Frantically, she made another left and was relieved to see the main street.

Daphne pushed her legs into a sprint. The street was still crowded. Her only hope was to try and disappear in the crowd. Sweat and tears stung her eyes. She wiped at her watery eyes just before she ran into a thick stone wall. She stopped herself with her palms.

"No. No!" She screamed in frustration. The wall had appeared in a matter of seconds. She could still hear the sounds of shoppers bustling on the other side. She pounded her hands against it. "Somebody, help me, please." She quickly searched for foot holds and found none. The wall was one gigantic smooth slab. She shook her head.

"Got you."

Daphne's shoulders sank in despair. She turned slowly and faced the posse that had chased her down one foreign street after another. They had Marcus hog tied. One of the boys was dragging him with a thick rope he had slung over his shoulder. His face was bleeding and one of his eyes was starting to turn dark blue.

"Please," she pleaded. She tried to back away, but the wall held her in place. "Just let us go."

"You should have stayed in your burrow spider," the leader sneered. His lips began to move as he muttered in a language she couldn't understand. His eyes glowed orange and a persimmon light began to swirl around his hands. He clenched his hands into fists and brought them level with his waist. A battle cry erupted and he charged.

Hot tears streaked down Daphne's face. "Holy Mary, Mother of God, pray for us sinners, now and at the hour of our death." As she sank to her knees as she prayed and made the sign of the cross.

Dauro pushed his right hand forward releasing a stream of orange energy. The light sped toward Daphne. It slammed into an invisible wall in front of her. The force of the two energies colliding sent bright red sparks flying in all directions. A wave of intense heat washed over her. The wind was so strong Daphne had to squint and turn her head. The boy threw another punch. Daphne felt as if she'd had the wind knocked out of her. She lay on the ground clutching her chest and gasping. Dauro stood over her and pulled his hand back as far as he could.

"I won't have trash like you walking my street." His hand flew forward and the magic burned out. "What the frell?" he looked down at his hand. He looked at his two companions, but they were already running in opposite directions. Fifteen men in dark blue capes and shining helmets were coming straight for them. The wall vanished and he jumped over Daphne and disappeared into the crowd.

"What is the meaning of this?" the squadron leader growled. He gestured to one of his men to untie Marcus, who'd been left lying in the street.

"It's nothing. Just a disagreement between wizards," Marcus answered.

"You vagabonds ought to be put in the stocks and whipped. Brawling in the streets is expressly forbidden."

He knelt down and fished around the inside of Marcus's collar with his fingers. He lifted the chain and looked at the symbol hanging from the boy's neck. The purple crystal was shaped like an olive tree and it had silver encased inside to showcase the branches.

"Laurels of Wisdom. No piercings means you're still an apprentice." He hauled Marcus to his feet and shook his head. "I expect better from one with your status. Your master will have to be told and you'll have to pay the fine."

"Of course. I understand," Marcus said. He hung his head and tried to look chagrinned.

"Sir," one of the Templar soldiers shouted. "You better have a look at this."

Marcus muttered a curse as the leader strolled toward Daphne. She was being held in place by three Templar soldiers. There was one on each side of her and another standing behind her with a firm grip on her hair. They had her on her knees. Her hands had been secured behind her back with magic handcuffs. A fourth soldier was working on shackling her ankles.

"Misunderstanding was it?" the leader asked, glaring over his shoulder at Marcus. He leaned down and looked at Daphne's face. He lifted her chin and turned her face from side to side. He looked into her eyes and shook his head. "I don't believe it," he breathed. "Tell me spider, what brings you out of your burrow?"

Daphne didn't respond. She locked her jaw and tried to tighten her stomach muscles. Her previous experience with the Templar caused her to instinctively tense up.

"What's the matter? Sporat got your tongue?" She didn't answer. "What's this?" He ran two fingers against the side of her neck and the cross necklace came into view. He bounced the gold cross in his hands and then let out a laugh. "Take the cuffs off."

"Sir?" the soldiers asked.

"She's not one of them." He stood and stretched. The bones in his back popped.

"Sir, are you certain?"

"I was working the prison transport when they brought her in."

"But sir—"

"Don't you morons read the scrolls? This girl's from another dimension."

"That protection spell she used was pretty impressive," another added nervously.

He shook his head. "It couldn't have been that great if a first year Dragon got the best of her." The cuffs were removed. He offered Daphne his hand and helped her to her feet.

"I apologize, but you can never be too careful when dealing with one of them."

"Does this mean I'm free to go?" she asked, rubbing her wrists.

"Oh no, you're still under arrest."

"What? But it wasn't our fault. Those creeps attacked us."

"I don't doubt it. It is what they do. The Dragons have certainly become more dauntless since your counterpart left us."

"All the more reason you should be going after them and not us."

"Nice try my dear. But you're still under arrest." He placed his hand on her shoulder.

"But—"

"Trust me. This is for your own good. Jasly, be sure to restrain the wizard."

"Wait." Marcus protested. "Why do I have to be hauled in like some common criminal?"

"Because you're dangerous."

CHAPTER 24

Daphne's new cell looked more like it belonged in a prison and less like the inside of a toaster oven. The bars were tangible steel beams. The corner of her cell had a pedestal sink with a frameless mirror above it. Hanging from the wall was a futon mattress on top of a flat sheet of metal. The metal bed was held in place by chains. A cheap white blanket lay folded at the foot of the bed. About 12 feet above her was a tiny window about the size of an index card. The starlight shone faintly through the bars. She tested the bed with her hands before climbing up. The chains squeaked and the bed sagged under her weight.

"Nothing like a metal hammock to lull you to sleep," the squadron leader joked as he closed the cell door and locked her in.

"How long do I have to stay here?" she asked.

"That depends."

"On what?"

"On how long it takes your master to bail you out."

"Great. I guess I shouldn't hold my breath then."

"I'm sure you'll be out soon. That wizard boy's release is already in progress."

"You're kidding. Ugh. That's just great," she seethed. "I don't see why I have to be in here. I didn't do anything. You even said I'm not dangerous."

"Not according to this," he said. He waved a small yellow card and tucked it in his pocket.

"What is that thing?"

"A list of your charges."

"Can I see it?"

"Of course, but I don't think it would do you much good."

"Why not?"

"As I understand it, they don't speak Runey where you're from."

"Well can you at least tell me what it says?"

"You're charged with disturbing the peace."

"That's all? Where I'm from I don't think they even arrest people for that. At most you get like community service or something."

"Kid I don't usually waste my time arresting people for fighting in the street either"

"Then why am I in here?"

"You're a special case. Just looking the way you do can incite a riot."

"It's not like I can change the way I look."

"And that's why you need to stay here. The trumped up charges give me a reason to keep you. Give the Dragons some time to calm down and then it should be safe for you to go out."

"I don't like being locked up."

"Just relax. You might actually enjoy yourself."

He walked slowly down the hall, looking in on each prisoner. He even checked the locks on the empty cells before shutting off the lights and locking them in for the night. Daphne groaned and lay on her side. The mattress was soft and smelled as if it'd been washed with Gain. With the interior lights off, the starlight shone even brighter. Yawning, Daphne rolled onto her other side. The bed seemed to sap what was left of her energy. Her eyes slid closed. She yawned again and fell asleep to the sound of her bed chains creaking.

"Laurels of Wisdom," a female soldier called.

"Over here," Marcus called.

"Your fine's been paid," she said.

She approached his cell and quickly unlocked it. Marcus followed her down the short hallway and through the security door. He signed for his belongings at a small window and was buzzed through another security door into the reception area.

"I don't understand. Has my master been notified?"

"There's no need," Veda answered.

She was wearing a black leotard covered in pink and silver glitter. Draped around her shoulders was a short cape that stopped mid-thigh. She'd exchanged her simple gold hoops for seven interconnected pink and white crystal earrings. The diamond stud had changed from clear to pink and the tassels were a mix of black and purple. The automatic lock clicked loudly as the female soldier closed the door, leaving Marcus standing in the lobby with the young wizard and the handful of guards manning the front entrance.

"Thank you."

"And don't worry about old Hilia. There's no official record you were ever here."

"How did you manage that?"

"I was forced to pay a rather large bribe," she said as she cast a displeased look at the soldiers behind the front desk. The two men avoided eye contact and shuffled papers around, pretending to look busy.

"I appreciate it, but can you afford this?"

"I was paid in advance so you shouldn't worry," she said as she flipped some of her hair out of her face.

"The effort might be wasted unless you can spring my friend as well."

"Oh her," she sighed. "Believe it or not, I tried. It's no good. They refused to let her out."

"Templar soldiers refused a bribe?" he asked as they walked out the front door and stepped onto the sidewalk.

"I'm just as shocked as you are. Marcus, I've got to get going, but before I do, I have to know if it's true."

"If what's true?"

"Jayme Ray from our old district said he saw you with a Katz. It wasn't that girl you brought to the Cooler was it?"

"That was her, but it's not how Jayme thinks."

"I knew there was a reason she had her eyes covered. Marcus, how could you? Consorting with their kind can get you killed."

"I haven't turned to a life of crime. It's not how it looks. She's not one of them."

"And I suppose it was just dumb misfortune that she was born with green eyes? Give me a break. You've turned traitor. Have you forgotten what those people did to us?"

"No."

"You must have or you wouldn't have forgotten where your loyalties lie."

"Veda, give me the chance to explain."

"I can't believe I paid your fine. You're a dirty liar."

"We've known each other our entire lives. I think I deserve the benefit of the doubt at least once."

"Fine. Let's hear it? What's the story?"

"You don't have time now. You'll be late for you show. But I promise if you make time tomorrow, I'll tell you everything."

"Alright. A late breakfast at my place. And you better tell me everything."

"I will, I promise."

"Oh and bring proof."

"Veda!"

"I may have put you through the ringer, but I still trust you. Jayme Ray's not so easily convinced." She unchained a motorcycle from a lamp post and slipped her leg over the side. Without looking, she recklessly leapt into oncoming traffic. She swerved around larger vehicles and disappeared from view as she made a left at the end of the block.

Marcus knew he looked out of place walking the empty streets at this hour. This section of town was favored among the wealthier wizards. His faded clothes were fraying at the edges and lacked any trace of glitter or sparkles. He checked the page where he'd copied Veda's address. Her apartment complex should be easy to spot. While he'd seen many high walls and ornate gates, he knew of only one place with Cherub statues lining the top of the wall.

Marcus had assisted in the design of the security measure in his first year. It was meant to hide the surveillance cameras and motion sensors. The top of the wall had been his idea. There were hidden treads that allowed the positions of the statues to shift randomly. This enabled the guards to maintain a constant view of the grounds while keeping thieves guessing.

He made sure his crystal pendant was showing. The gate automatically swung open as he approached. It was a short walk to the front door of the nearest building. He checked the page he'd copied Veda's address onto. Her place was on the ground floor, the last apartment on the right. He rang the bell, waited two minutes, and rang it again. He could hear the deadbolt snap and the jingling of chains as she undid the security latch.

"You're early," she said sleepily. She held the door slightly ajar.

"The master has me on a short leash for the next few days. I'm lucky he even agreed to let me out for this."

She opened the door wide enough for him to enter and quietly closed it. She quickly reset all the locks and made a shooing motion in the direction of the sofa. He took a seat while she put on a pot of tea. The furniture was simple, but not cheap. While it lacked a pattern, the deep purple sofa was made of some of the most expensive fabric available in the realm of Hambly. The thick white carpet had been covered with a large black area rug. A few framed pieces of art had been hung on the walls. Solid black curtains covered the windows. The only light in the room came from table lamps. The cream colored lamp shades made it easy for soft white light to fill the space.

"Make yourself at home," she said, still groggy. She was still wearing the sparkling leotard and cape he'd seen her in the night before. She'd taken all her piercings out and washed off her makeup. Her skin carried a pale green tint. With half open eyes, she leaned against the counter and gazed in his general direction.

"Don't take this the wrong way, but you look terrible."

"I was out late. It's true what they say. Royalty tips big. But what they don't tell you is that they work you worse than Pegasi slaves."

"You're exaggerating."

"No, she's not either," another woman said, shuffling into the living room from one of the bedrooms. She pulled her robe tightly around her neck and searched the dishwasher for a clean cup. Her bleach blonde hair was tousled from sleep. There were black circles around her eyes and red smudges on the side of her face, proof that she'd fallen asleep with her makeup on.

"There were three of us and it still wasn't enough. Poor Sazarah was pushed to the limit. I tried to warn her to take it easy, but her nose was already bleeding."

"Is she alright?" Marcus asked.

"I hope so. She had to be rushed to the hospital after. They think she ruptured a blood vessel in her brain."

"Wow," he breathed. The tea kettle started whistling. Veda added a few loose leaves and lifted the pot off the stove.

"So what's this I hear about you turning traitor?" the other woman asked as she placed three cups on the counter. "I would think green eyes would turn your stomach after what happened last time." Marcus clenched his teeth and frowned.

"Let it go Ameera," Veda said sleepily. "We've all been suckered in by a pretty face at least once. Did you ever get your father's emblem back?"

"No. It's been so long they probably melted it down and sold it already."

"I wouldn't count on that," Veda said, perking up slightly with her first sip of tea. "The green eyed spiders are known for keeping trophies."

"Let's get to the business at hand," Ameera said, sliding a cup across the counter toward Marcus, "What's with you and this girl you got arrested for."

"It's just as I said, Jayme Ray and Dauro have the wrong idea. Daphne is not a Katz. She's just unlucky." Marcus rose and joined them in the kitchen. He slowly drank half the tea in his cup aware that they were losing patience with him at every sip. He quickly went through the story as he knew it.

"A case of mistaken identity?" Veda asked. Her skin was a glowing white and had lost its sickly green luster. "So, what proof do you have for us? I mean, if you want the message to get around that the green eyed devils are short their most powerful game piece, I need something to take to Jayme Ray and the others."

He reached into his jacket and produced an envelope. He laid it on the counter.

"What's this?" Veda asked.

"It's Daphne's hunter contract."

"Why do you have it?" her roommate snapped.

"I'm supposed to read it to her and make sure she signs it."

He sipped his tea as Veda carefully opened the sealed envelope. The two women leaned their heads together while they read. After a long span of silence, Veda carefully folded the pages and slipped them back inside the envelope. She took a stick of glue from a drawer beneath the counter and slid it along the seal. She pressed the seal closed and held it up to the light to make sure there were no signs of tampering before handing it back to him.

"Well?" Marcus asked.

"It certainly looks real enough," Ameera sighed.

"I'm satisfied. And needless to say, very impressed." Veda spoke softly. "Hyron signed his real name and it has Master Raven's signet."

"It doesn't make sense. You say this girl can't even gather light energy. Yet she gets a blessing to study magic from the Guardians of the Forbidden. It's all a little too suspicious, don't you think?"

"Who are the guardians of the forbidden?" Veda asked.

"They're some of the most powerful guild masters in the tri-system. Rumor has it that the council members are chosen every year by the emperor. They always sign with the seal of Master Raven."

"They always sign?" Marcus asked. "There's only one stamp here."

Ameera shrugged. "I've heard that each of the guardians possesses a portion of the stamp. They can only sign when they are all together and agree."

"And they chose to agree on here? What do you think it means?" Veda asked.

Ameera shrugged and scraped glitter from her forehead. "If I wanted to play detective, I would have become a soldier or joined a hunters guild." She yawned and gently placed her empty cup in the sink. "I'm exhausted. I'm going back to bed. And so should you," she said to Veda. "You have two shows in the afternoon and another tonight."

Veda groaned. "Of course. Marcus, you can see yourself out can't you?"

CHAPTER 25

"Rise and shine," the squadron leader called.

The interior lights flashed on. He was greeted with several groans and a few curses. In his hand was a folded packet of paper. He was being followed by a little boy wheeling a cart stacked with five covered metal trays. Daphne sat up and yawned. She'd been awake for hours and watched the sunrise through her tiny window. The squadron leader oversaw a young boy in a cape-less Templar uniform as he slid trays of food and bowls of water across the floor and through the middle of bars. Daphne hopped off her bed and touched the bars. They still felt solid.

The squadron leader laughed. "Kid, only you would still be impressed by a parlor trick like that."

"I just want to know how he does it."

"Kid, that's basic magic. Phasing through objects is something they teach in preschool."

"I do have a name you know."

He ignored her. "Good job son," he said to the boy. "Go see if Master Iba has any work for you."

"Yes Mr. Jerrick."

"It's lieutenant commander or sir. Learn your ranks or you'll be serving slop for the rest of your life."

"Yes sir." The boy pushed open the door at the end of the hall and slipped out of sight.

"Jerrick," Daphne said. "Is that your first name or your last name?"

He rolled his eyes and sat in a chair near the cell across from hers. He unfolded the paper and started reading.

"Is that the Daily Scroll?" Daphne asked. He loudly turned the page and lifted the paper high enough to shield his face from view. "Why do you leave us unattended all night and then come sit with us in the morning? Any person with half a brain would try to escape at night."

He put folded the paper and set it noisily on his lap. "Do you mind? I'm trying to read."

"You could make things easier for yourself if you just tried to make conversation."

"I don't get paid to talk to prisoners. In fact, it's strongly discouraged."

"I'm going to keep asking you until you give me an answer," Daphne said.

"Fine," he growled. "It's common knowledge that prison breaks usually happen during the day when most of the soldiers are on patrol. Jerrick is my first name, my favorite color is blue, yes I like my job, and not that you asked, but I like reading the paper in silence. Anything else?"

She shook her head no.

"Why are you so curious anyway?"

Daphne shrugged. "I'm just trying to learn everything I can about this place. When I go home, I want to tell my mom all about it. And most of the other prisoners are gone. You're really the only person left to talk to."

He sighed. "It's already been four days. Is your master ever going to bail you out?"

"I wouldn't get my hopes up if were you. I'm likely to die of old age before that cheap skate pays storage and fees for me."

"I'm willing to drop all the charges and forgive the fine if he'll just take you away. I feel guilty keeping you locked up knowing I'd take more damage from a paper cut."

"Do I have your word on that?" Steele asked. He strolled in escorted by the boy who brought and cleared the meal trays.

"Yes. I was this close to letting the Dragons finish her off just to put me out of my misery."

"Nice. That's real noble of you," Daphne said sarcastically.

"What took you so long anyway?" Jerrick asked. "I was starting to think you hadn't gotten the message."

"Oh, I got the message," Steele said.

Daphne rolled her eyes. "And you just let me sit here?"

Steele shrugged. She growled and tried to jiggle the bars. "Are you going to unlock the door and let me out or not?"

"Gladly." Jerrick rose from his seat and slipped the key in the lock. He and Daphne both breathed a sigh of relief as the locked clicked and the door slid open.

"Ah, sweet freedom," she said.

"Hey kid," Jerrick said. "A word of advice. Whether you think you're a Katz or not makes no difference. If you want to stay alive, stay out of Dragon territory. If anyone has the biggest score to settle with the infamous Spider Guild, it's them." He led them down the hall and held open the security door.

"I'll do my best. Not that I know where Dragon territory is. And what do they have against the Katzes anyway? I mean, I get that no one likes the Katz family. They're probably like your planet's version of Al Qaeda, but what do the Dragons have against them? What did they do? Marcus told me about that war, but that was centuries ago."

"The Katzes have had their hand in every shred of criminal activity since they lost the revolution," Steele volunteered. "They maintain power by staying out of sight and ruling with an iron fist from behind the scenes. If they ever venture out in public, they go in disguise. The green eyes are pretty obvious."

"So I've been told."

"Of course," Jerrick interjected, "what's not in the history books is that when the Katz clan lost the war, those who didn't die on the battlefield suffered from persecution. They were hunted down like animals. If they were caught, they were as good as dead.

Their numbers are so small now I think most people have given up on blood feuds."

"Most people, except the Dragons?" Daphne ventured. "Why?"

Jerrick shrugged. "I couldn't tell you. But what I can tell you is where there are honest people, there are always swindlers and thieves. Territory lines are clearly drawn and understood. Your double crossed that line and stole power from the Dragons. Ever since, she's had her foot on the neck of almost every crime syndicate and lower class citizen in the tri-system."

"And now that she's out of the picture, everyone's fighting for their piece of the pie?" Daphne asked.

"In a way. That sorceress combined criminal guilds for the first time. She wasn't satisfied with a little piece of something. She wanted it all. And now that's she's gone, it's a war to see who gets it." He paused to unlock another security door. "I don't know if I should be telling you this or not," Jerrick said. He looked Daphne up and down as if he were sizing her up. "I suppose you couldn't do that much harm with it."

"What do you know?" Steele asked.

"Rumor has it that all the criminal guilds signed a treaty. They plan on erasing any trace of the Katz bloodline. There's even been talk of trying to seal the portal to .835 when it opens just to keep that woman from coming back."

"They can't really do that can they?" Daphne asked.

Jerrick shrugged. "Theoretically, anything's possible."

Dr. Ouji hunched over the two open files on his desk. He scratched his scalp in frustration. He closed his eyes and rubbed his temples before finally pushing his chair back. He closed the files and shoved them in a desk drawer. He yawned, reached for his coffee and changed his mind. His office door swished open and his assistant entered carrying a box of computer files. The collection of colored computer chips glittered like a rainbow.

"This is the last of them," she said, adding the box to the top of a stack in the corner.

"Thank you Helena."

"Doctor, do you mind if I ask what you're looking for? Perhaps I could be of assistance." She was poised eagerly on the balls of her feet, hoping he'd say yes.

"Oh, it's nothing for you to worry about. I was just doing some research," he said. He began to sort through the boxes of computer chips cluttering his office. One look at her disappointed face and he knew he would waiver and let her help him.

"For your petition to the high court at Manyx?"

"How did you know about that?" he asked.

He stopped arranging files and looked over his shoulder. Her black hair had been pulled back into a short ponytail. The look showed off the features of her face. She was an attractive young girl. Her brown skin sparkled despite the horrible lighting in his office. The sheepish smile on her face caused the skin under her eyes to wrinkle slightly. The wrinkling drew attention the fact that her eyes were two different colors: brown and green. The bright green drew attention to the baldly scarred skin of her left eye.

"I was only told this morning that I'd been granted an audience. Frankly, I'm surprised they're even agreeing to see me. I'm used to being ignored."

"One of my siblings is a clerk for the High Guardian."

"You never told me that."

"He only graduated into the position this year. He always lets me know when something interesting happens."

"Really?"

"Uh huh. As a matter of fact, in his last letter, he shared an interesting bit of information about that girl who looked like the sorceress Katz."

Ouji stopped digging. His eyes widened and turned his eyes on Helena. "Really. What did he say?"

"You needn't worry doctor, she's still alive."

"That's good." He breathed a sigh of relief and his eyes slowly shrank to a normal size.

"That depends on your definition of good."

"Well, go on then."

"It seems she was arrested."

"What for?"

"Public brawling. There was an incident involving the Dragons. They attacked. She and the young wizard she was with defended themselves. Of course, the Templar took her in for disturbing the peace and let the actual perpetrators go. Despite that, the Guardians of the Forbidden gave their blessing to Guild Master Hyron. As soon as Daphne signs the contract, she'll be Realms Honor's first official apprentice."

"I wonder why it had to go all the way to the central palace. Surely the emperor's underlings don't spend their time approving apprentice applications. I always thought apprentice selections were handled locally?" he mused. "Then again, I spend so much time cooped up in this office, what do I really know about policy?"

"Under normal circumstances, you'd be correct."

"Then why—"

"It's the green eyes." She spoke with a level of resigned acceptance. "Any sign of Katz blood automatically requires royal approval if you need a high security clearance."

"I see. Then you as well?"

"Healer's academy handled my application internally. The healer's guilds are very open about judging a person on their merits and not their family heritage. I only needed approval for my residency under a master because you work with high security prison transports."

"What about your brother? I would think that the royal house would deny someone with even a small trace of Katz blood palace access."

"I'm adopted. For whatever reason, the Katz family abandoned me. I was fortunate to be just beyond the boundaries of Dragon territory when I was found."

"I see."

"If there's nothing else sir I'll—"

"Helena?"

"Sir?"

"I could use some help with this report. Do you mind sorting these files and compiling the data for me?"

"Of course. I'll start on it right away."

"It'll have to be later this evening. We're about to make the pass into West Valeri. The portal to .927 just closed and I've been told they're bringing in a second capture. They caught him using old access codes trying to sneak into this dimension."

"I suppose the first capture will be relieved. His record will be cleared."

"It's been over 10 years Helena. I don't think it really makes a difference to the other man whether his conviction gets overturned."

"Why not? Everyone loves a clean slate."

"Because, he's already dead."

"Does that mean the guilty one will just go free?"

"That's how it usually works."

"What about the double execution?"

"All double executions have been suspended until the committee votes on my proposal. He'll likely just sit in prison for a while until a large enough bribe can buy his freedom."

"Can't we do something? It just doesn't seem right that he doesn't have to pay for his crimes."

Dr. Ouji shook his head. "Our task is to treat his wounds and shield him from mistreatment until justice is served."

"How do you stand it? Watching people die needlessly. How do you hold on to your sense of morality and your compassion? What keeps you from using your skills to fix things yourself?"

"Helena, when you allow yourself to become judge and jury, you start to believe you know more than you do. You give yourself more power than you should and you do things you can't take back. The kind of guilt can drive a man insane."

She shuddered at the dark shadow that had taken over his once sparkling eyes. He swept his cape off the coat hanger and pinned it to the shoulders of his uniform. He lifted his medical bag off the floor and began filling it with supplies from the cabinets. What's your secret doctor, she wondered. Where does your guilt lie?

CHAPTER 26

The doorbell rang. There was a knock. Emory wiped a sweaty hand on his trousers. There was another knock, louder this time. The sound spurred him toward the door. As he grasped the doorknob he tensed his muscles in an effort to stay the trembling in his hand. The doorknob felt slimy against his palm. He rubbed his hand dry again and opened the door.

Agent Johnston stood squarely in the doorway. His black suit had been pressed and was free of lint. His dark hair had a fresh sheen to it. His square jaw was clean shaven. The lack of facial hair made his pale skin look sickly. The skin around short fingernails was dry and white. His cuticles were cracking, a sign that he had a tendency to bite his nails. Beside him was a much younger man with fair hair and blue eyes. The younger agent's hands were pink and his nails appeared to have been manicured.

In their black suits and polished black shoes they looked like the stereotypical federal agents from movies and TV. Behind them he could see several black SUVs and black sedans positioned along the street. Two agents had positioned themselves at the bottom of the porch steps. Two others stood quietly by each side of the front door. He assumed that others were guarding the back and side entrances. The younger one fiddled with his glasses before he spoke.

"May we come in?" Agent Isles asked.

"Yes," Addison said. Her voice betrayed her eagerness. Her bloodshot eyes and the new wrinkles on her face were signs she'd spent too many sleepless nights worrying and waiting. She flanked the opposite side of the door. She was leaned against the doorframe with a twisted paper towel in her hands. She was unconsciously twisting and tearing tiny pieces. The living room carpet was covered in tiny white flakes.

The agents stepped inside and the door was shut firmly behind them. There was the sound of shoes scraping against wood as the agents by the door shifted their positions. Addison slipped into a chair, her fingers still fumbling with the napkin. Emory gestured for the agents to sit. He remained standing and took a position behind his wife. He rested his hands on her thin, trembling shoulders.

"Mr. and Mrs. Morrow," Agent Johnston began, "what I'm about to tell you is extremely classified information. I must warn you that it may not provide you with the answers you're looking for."

"I understand," Emory said. His voice was emotionless. He squeezed Addison's shoulders. For a brief moment they stopped shaking. "Please."

"After months of investigation, we have come to the conclusion that your daughter was in fact taken by a form of intelligence not native to this planet."

"You're not serious," Emory breathed. He grabbed onto the back of his wife's chair for support. Hearing this from one of the men who'd laughed in his face not so long ago made him feel as though the wind had been knocked out of him.

"We are very sorry," Agent Isles added. "But given the circumstances of Daphne's abduction—"

"No." Addison interrupted. "There must be something you can do."

"Ma'am I'm very sorry."

"No! I won't accept that. Decades of research and exploration and technological development—all those tax dollars and all you can say to me is I'm sorry?"

"Ma'am please," Agent Isles urged calmly.

"No. I refuse to accept that that's it. You have to know something. There has to be something you can do. I want my daughter back!"

"Well we believe that whatever this thing is chose your family for a reason. Obviously there was something special about your daughter," Agent Johnston said.

"What? What could these things possibly want with our daughter?"

"We don't know. It's possible they only took her for," he let his voice trail off and let the words hang in the air. He knew their imaginations would fill in the blanks.

"So that's it then?" Emory breathed. He wandered toward the piano. Like a man in a trance, his feet drug across the floor. His trembling fingers wrapped around the edge of a framed picture of a young Daphne. Tears silently fell onto the glass protecting the photo.

"No. That's not it!" Addison screamed. "It can't be."

"This may seem callous of me to ask, but if you and your husband would be willing to submit to some tests, perhaps we could—."

"No." Emory said firmly.

"Yes!" Addison responded frantically. She turned to look at her husband. "Yes," she said the word as a command.

"No," Emory said, turning to face his wife.

"Yes," she said again, turning back to the agent. "We'll all do it. Galen, Dylan, and myself."

"Unfortunately because your husband was adopted, your nephew and your brother-in-law wouldn't be of any use to us."

"Addie, think about what you're doing," Emory urged. "It's not worth it. It won't bring her back to us."

"I don't care. If I never see her again, I don't care. But I have to know why."

"Ma'am, you should listen to your husband," Agent Isles said softly. "Take some time and consider what you're agreeing to."

"I know what you're asking."

"Addison stop," Emory ordered. "It's over. She's gone." He could tell she was ignoring him. "Listen to me. She wouldn't want you to waste your life like this."

"Whatever it takes. If there's even a 1 percent chance I can see my Daphne again, I want to try."

Agent Isles looked from Addison to Emory. The expressions on each of their faces were very different. The father was obviously grief stricken. Tears cascaded silently down his face and his body shook. He was barely able to contain himself. It seemed that at any moment he would be crushed under the weight of all he had endured these past few months.

The woman's face had taken on a vacant, drone like expression. All the light seemed to have vanished from her eyes. Her gaze was fixed on some invisible focal point over his shoulder. Isles turned his head and followed her frozen stare. He was almost hoping to see whatever invisible thing had gripped her soul. The paper towel had dropped from her fingers. Her body and voice no longer trembled. She spoke in a commanding monotone.

"Mrs. Morrow," Agent Isles tried again. "You should take some time to think—"

"I don't need to think. I want you to tell me what I need to do."

"You do understand that in this process, there are no guarantees," Agent Johnston said.

"I don't care. It's for my Daphne. I'll do anything."

"I can't believe you," Marcus laughed. "This is beyond pathetic to watch."

"Shut up!" Daphne snapped.

"You've been at it all morning. You should take a break," Kember said, setting a plate of finger sandwiches on the table.

"I don't get it," Marcus said, stuffing his face. "That protection spell you used against that Dragon kid was amazing and now you can't even make a simple light spark."

"That was different," Daphne argued.

"Well explain it to me, because I'm hopelessly lost."

"I can't. I don't know how it happened. I was just…I just really didn't want to die."

"Well let's hope you don't need a life or death situation to be useful," Steele said, entering the room. He shifted the backpack he was carrying to his other shoulder. "What, no screams of terror?" he asked, kicking off his boots. As the shoes bounced off the baseboard of the nearest wall, he wrapped an arm around Kember's waist and planted a kiss on her neck. She giggled and playfully pushed him away.

Daphne shrugged. "No. I've kind of gotten used to you sneaking up on me." She nibbled on the corner of a sandwich and turned the pages in one of her study manuals. She mumbled the words aloud as she stumbled over the Runey symbols. Marcus grabbed two more sandwiches and took up his usual position on his back as he ate.

"Here," Steele said. Daphne's concentration broke as he placed her mp3 player on top of the page. Her eyes widened. She looked from him to Marcus. The surprise on her face quickly turned to irritation.

"Why you," she growled. She grabbed a dictionary and beaned her tutor on the side of his head.

"Hey!" He sat up and coughed as a chunk of bread slid down the wrong tube.

"What the heck is this?" she snapped, brandishing the tiny device like a weapon.

"Thanks a lot Steele."

The bounty hunter chuckled as he sauntered into the kitchen. He listened to Daphne verbally attack Marcus. The boy attempted to defend himself between fits of coughing, but even on a good day Marcus was no match for Daphne's trademark sarcasm. An open bottle of beer was already on the counter waiting for him. He took two long drafts before returning to the living room.

Kember was sitting in a chair. She had her body turned so that the chair arms were cradling her. She had an open book propped against her thighs and carefully turned the pages with a bandaged hand. Marcus cringed like a wounded animal as Daphne wagged a glowing finger dangerously close to his face.

"Don't you think he's had enough kid?" Steele asked.

"I'll decide when he's had enough. I've had it up to here with this dirty little trickster and his—" She stopped talking and stared at her hand. A small amount of light spiraled down her arm like a white mist and collected into a concentrated bright ball balanced on the tip of her pointer finger. "What the—?" she asked, spreading her fingers out and turning her hand palm upward to examine her fingers. The light quickly dissipated.

"It seems to me like you're finally getting the hang of it," Steele said.

"I guess so," she said still staring at her hand. For a brief moment, a smile crossed her face. She seemed to be looking at Steele and he smiled and nodded. As quickly as it appeared, her smile faded. Her gaze seemed to pass through him and into empty space. He couldn't help but feel sorry for her as a dark shadow took residence on her face. She settled back onto the couch, all the spirit drained out of her.

"Marcus, I guess you're forgiven," she said. He grinned sheepishly and she flashed him a weak smile.

"You're tired. Let's call it a day," Marcus offered.

"Sure."

"And don't worry about the verb conjugations," he said as he gathered his things. "You get a free pass today."

"Ooh, one day off. Thanks slave driver."

"You earned it." He threw his leather messenger strap over his shoulder. His joints groaned as he got out of a cross-legged position. The blood in his legs tingled as he stood after spending hours sitting on the floor. "Bye Daphne." She gave him a two finger salute and he quietly closed the door behind him.

CHAPTER 27

Daphne opened her eyes. She was in her room. She sighed. She must have fallen asleep on the couch again. Instead of leaving her to freeze until she woke up on her own like usual, Steele must have carried her to her room. She pushed back the heavy blanket that had been draped over her. The light coming through her window wasn't as bright today. The moons were out of sight and most of the stars were hidden behind clouds.

Daphne gently rubbed sleep from her eyes, stretched and yawned. She fished her new shoes from beneath the bed and crept down the stairs. A lamp had been left on, giving her enough light to navigate around the furniture and find the door. She unlocked the front door and stepped onto the porch before slipping her shoes on her feet. The air was cool but still warmer than the temperature inside. She crossed her arms and looked up into the blackish-blue night. The top edges of the clouds glowed like amethyst in the starlight. She closed her eyes and breathed in the warm air. She still hadn't learned to tell when it was late evening or early morning.

She didn't hear his footsteps but something told her someone was out there. Daphne turned her head and opened her eyes. She did her best to act calm. The fact was she hadn't expected him to be this close to her. And she had expected Steele. Instead, the man beside her was a stranger.

In the low light seeping onto the porch she could tell he stood a few inches shorter than Steele. He wore his golden brown hair long and had it swept back into a ponytail. His clothing was fancy, much like a wizard's, but it lacked all the overly showy frills. The small amount of gold filigree hadn't been adorned with crystals or glitter. His black cape was long and stopped short of dragging the ground. He wore leather gloves and he had a tiny scar under his chin. Around his neck was a multilayered pendant. There was a giant gold star and centered on it was a griffin perched on top of a shiny blue gemstone. The edges of the star framed the griffin like a golden five-sided halo. She knew the signal well. Steele wore the same one. The pendant never left his neck.

"Good evening Daphne," he said.

"I'm sorry, do I know you?"

"What, no hello?"

"You don't need to know him," Steele snapped. "You'll be better off."

"Harsh," the man said with mock chagrin.

"What are you doing here Cinnamon?"

"It seems you and I have some business to discuss."

"Daphne, go back to your room."

"If you two are going to talk about me, I think I'd like to stay."

"Don't worry, this has nothing to do with you," Cinnamon said.

"Why do I not believe you?" she asked narrowing her eyes at him.

"Daphne," Steele urged.

"Alright, alright, I'm going." She walked slowly toward the stairs. She didn't have to look back to know that Steele wasn't going to let Cinnamon in the house. The moment she stepped back inside, he'd positioned himself in center of the doorway. She heard the door close as she passed Kember on the stairs.

"What's going on?" Kember asked.

"Guild business I suppose," she said.

Downstairs Steele folded his arms across his chest. His frown deepened the wider the other's smug smile grew. Cinnamon slowly removed one glove and then the other. He tucked them in his belt and spread his hands in a non-threatening gesture.

"Let's make this clear," Steele said. "I wouldn't have called you if there was any other guild member I could pass this along too."

"I know."

"And don't think I don't know that you pulled one of your usual tricks. I'm sick of this twisted game of yours, paying off everyone to turn me down so I'd be forced to come to you."

Cinnamon's smile widened until he was showing teeth. He laughed in Steele's face. "If you're so clever, then why do I always manage to catch you in my trap?"

"Trust me, if I could have gone to another guild, I would have."

"And why didn't you?"

"The request came from the 9th house of Valeri. They were insistent that the task be completed by a member of Realms Honor."

"I see."

"What are the terms?" Steele asked.

"Tsk, tsk Steele. Aren't you going to invite me in?"

"No. I want this over and done with."

"Always to the point with you." Cinnamon paused and looked at the sky. The clouds had begun to shift and more stars were peeking through. "What do you suppose fascinates that apprentice of yours so?" he asked gesturing to the sky. "She's out here almost every night you know. Starring at the vastness of space as if the answers to all her questions are spelled out in the heavens."

"What are the terms?" Steele asked again.

"I want the girl."

"No."

"And why not? I take this job off your hands so you two can go on your little camping trip and when you get back, you give her to me."

"No."

"Steele, Steele, Steele. Why so stubborn? Keep this up and you'll only drag out her misery and your own. Even a blind man can see you two can't stand each other. You never wanted her to begin with, so what does it matter if I take her off your hands?"

"Nothing you touch ever turns out well for anyone but yourself."

"I fail to see how that's a bad thing."

"Name something else. I'll pay you whatever you ask, but you can't have her."

"Fine, then I'll buy her contract from you. Name your price."

"I said no. I won't sell her to you or anyone."

"This is your last chance. Give me the girl or I'll go to Hyron."

"Ha. You're more desperate than I thought if you think father will go back on his own order if you pout and throw a little money around."

"Get your head out of the clouds! There's no place in the world for men like you and that prison doctor. High morals are for the ignorant and cowards too afraid to get their hands dirty."

"Are you going to take the job or not?"

"What if I say no?"

"Then I'll be forced to take her with me."

"You wouldn't."

"I would if it meant keeping her from you."

"You can't take a girl like her into the Skyfall! She'd—."

"That's right. And if she dies you'll never get what you're after."

Cinnamon clenched and unclenched his fists. His jaw trembled and he pressed his molars together until his jaw hurt. "Fine. Have it your way. I'll take the job."

"What are the terms?" Steele asked.

"No charge." Cinnamon relaxed as his brother's smug smile vanished and his eyebrows went up.

"No charge?"

"It's what I said isn't it?" He held out his hand and Steele passed him a small yellow computer file. Cinnamon tucked the chip in his shirt pocket. "Don't worry. I'll perform the task with all the discretion and dignity of my rank."

"I expect nothing less."

"What's the matter Steele? You seem surprised."

"I was just wondering what goes on in that little brain of yours."

"You won't trade her and you won't sell her, what other choice do I have?"

"It's not like you to give up."

"No. It's not. Hyron'll rescind the order and assign her to me. You'll make sure of that."

"As Daphne says, don't hold your breath."

"Good night Steele." He gave his brother a two finger salute and vanished in the thickness of the forest.

"Again!" Steele shouted. He whacked Daphne across the backside with a wooden cane. She gave him her most hateful look. She wiped her hands on her pants and tightened the strap holding back her hair before crouching into a starting position. She took a deep breath and counted slowly.

"One, two, go!" she took off running full tilt toward the obstacle course. Instead of running head on for the wooden climbing wall, this time she made a slight detour and jumped on a rock. One foot landed on the top of the stone and she used the other to bounce off the ground. The extra bit of leverage gave her more height. She smashed against the wall, but instead of missing the hand holds and sliding into the dust, her fingers managed to hold on and she scrambled to the top.

She sprang off the wall. A sudden wind blew and the rope she was aiming for was blown out of reach. She tucked and rolled before hitting the ground. Steele shook his head as she ended up on her back. The rope swung above her face, the tips of some of the strands brushing against her nose.

"Pathetic," he said.

"Why do I even have to do this? I thought I was supposed to focus on magic."

"A strong body is the foundation to strong magical power. You need stamina. You have to know what it's like to take a beating and keep going. Magic can't be your only avenue. Do it again."

"What? I've done this 100 times already." she whined.

"Do it again."

Her shoulders and arms ached from the strain of trying to lift her own weight. While her legs reveled to have activity again, her knees were tender from all the rough landings. She fought to walk without limping. And she was sure there were bruises all over her back. Her heart hammered against the inside of her chest. She gasped for air and wiped sweat from her forehead. Her shirt was soaked and she was covered in dust. She looked down at her wrists. She ran the fingers of one hand over her skin. The tiny scabs left from the scratches caused by her father had finally faded. Her skin was perfect and without scars.

She licked her lips and took in the obstacle course again. There was a wooden climbing wall with hand and foot holds carved into it. After the wall was one rope. She was supposed to swing on it and into a nearby tree. Once in the tree, the goal was to hop from the tip of one branch to the branches of another tree on the other side of the clearing. Then she was supposed to swing on another rope toward the river and drop onto a post sticking out of the water. She then had to hop the line of posts to the other side, fetch a gemstone from a basket and swim back. So far, Daphne hadn't made it past the climbing wall. And since she couldn't swim, she wasn't sure how she was supposed to complete that last step.

"Ahem," Steele said. "Get on with it."

"What's the rush? I've got all day don't I?"

"If by all day you mean 36 hours, then sure. But I was under the impression you liked your sleep."

"You're not going to make me do this in the dark."

"I already told you, do the whole thing at least once before day's end."

She laughed and shook her head. The youthful sound rang out like a bell. Birds chirped in response from their hiding places. Her dark brown girls bounced. In the afternoon sunlight some of her hair glowed a dusty golden color. Her green eyes sparkled like two gemstones.

"This is insane," Daphne said. "I can't believe he was right."

Steele watched as she flexed and stretched before crouching to make another attempt. Her demeanor had changed. She'd shed her reluctance and seemed to be working to impress someone only she could see.

"Who're you talking about?" Steele asked.

"My dad. He's teaches science at the university and you wouldn't know it to look at him, but he's like you."

"Like me? How?"

"Fit, you know?" she said standing and stretching. "He was always on my case, saying I should make an effort to be more athletic. That it just might save my life. If he were here, I know he'd gloat. He couldn't resist. He'd be standing over there saying I told you so."

"Don't you just hate it when parents are right?"

"Hey, I didn't live a completely sedentary life you know. I exercised."

Steele rolled his eyes. "I'm sure competitive ballroom dancing wasn't what your father hand in mind."

"How'd you know?"

"Have you forgotten you live in my house? I'd have to be a fool not to notice the way you flit and bounce around when you think no one's watching."

"Well, here goes nothing," she said. She shifted her body back into a racer's starting pose. Her muscles more relaxed this time. She used her fingertips to push her upper body up and forward. Her legs moved like two springs. This time, she skipped the rock and managed to spring up the wall to the first handhold on her own.

"You know," she said, straining to pull herself up, "I don't hate that he was right. I hate that I didn't listen sooner. If I had, maybe I would have been able to hold onto him and that column a little longer."

When she reached the top of the wall, she ran along the edge and built up a little speed. She jumped for the rope and was able to grab on at a higher point. She slid down it a little as her body's force carried it toward the tree. Steele couldn't help but smile as she leapt elegantly from one tree to into the cradling branches of another. Daphne grunted as her armpits slapped against the fork shaped branches. There was a different energy coming from her as she landed on the first river post. She hopped to the far shore, retrieved the stone and instead of trying to swim back, she tried to use the wooden posts to cross the small river again.

The post dropped into the water. The river was shallow enough that the water didn't cover her head and weak current prevented her from being swept downstream. He laughed as she floundered around in neck deep water. Each time she grabbed onto one of the wooden posts, it would quickly drop below the surface. He was still laughing when she hauled herself onto the bank. Her disdainful look was back.

"How was your bath?" he chuckled.

"Bite me," she snapped. She threw the gemstone at his feet and wrung out her hair. He offered her his hand. She smacked it away and stood on her own. She wiped her muddy hands on her wet pants.

"Good job, looks like we'll still have time to hike back to the campsite before it gets dark."

"You're kidding."

He was already walking deeper into the forest. "You know how to pitch a tent and make a fire don't you?" he called.

"And the Templar thought I was evil," she muttered.

CHAPTER 28

Hyron lit another cigar. After a long drag of the earthy tasting smoke, he turned his attention back to the stack of papers on his desk. He'd finished processing all the new open cases into the guild mainframe. He still had to read the recent pay requests from members who completed their missions and compare them with all the damage reports. There was also the matter of submitting his overdue tax forms to the Royal Bank of Valeri and delivering his annual report to the guardian of the realm.

"I hate paperwork," he said to the silence. "What I wouldn't give for youth and one more murderer or thief to hunt."

He ran his hand along his thigh. Hidden just behind the seam in his pants was a pocket where he kept his favorite knife. It wasn't anything fancy. The blade was smooth and sharp. The hilt was made from palladium, one of the more common metals in the tri-system. He rolled his hand around and flipped his wrist outward. Thin metal needles flew from their hiding place and landed around the center of a dart board.

"You're getting rusty old man," Cinnamon said as he strolled through the open office door. He carefully retrieved the metal spikes and laid them on the guild master's desk. "You missed the bull's eye."

"It's after hours Cinnamon, so you must want something."

"Like you father, I was just feeling nostalgic."

"If you don't have anything important to discuss, get out. I have a lot of work to do."

"Then I'll be brief. It's about the girl."

"No."

"You don't even know what I was going to ask."

"You want me to reassign her from Steele and give her to you. And the answer is no."

"Did he warn you I was coming?"

"Don't insult my intelligence Cinnamon. I didn't get to where I am on luck alone. My body may be old but I still have my connections and my wits. I know you were the one who bought her out of execution. I know that it was your money that forced Steele's inquiry. Were you hoping to find some skeleton in your brother's closet that would shift things in your favor?"

"I take back what I said. You obviously haven't lost your touch father. You're six steps ahead of Steele. He doesn't seem to have the faintest idea."

"Don't assume that because he hasn't approached you directly that he hasn't been investigating things. We don't all operate in the open."

"Perhaps, but surely you would agree that the guild and the girl would benefit from a master with more documented success."

"Steele is doing a fine job. Until now, he's never made a mistake with a case."

"But wouldn't you agree Daphne's level of improvement is far below the usual standard."

"Considering her background, that can be over looked. In a year she'll be ready for on the job training."

"A year? Too much can happen in a year. If you know what I mean."

"I'm not in the mood for your games. By law, the girl is Steele's responsibility."

"Yes but—"

"Don't expect me to get in the middle of this. I won't betray one son to another for a little bit of coin. As guild master, I've done my duty by gaining royal approval for her training. Her contract has been signed and processed. She belongs to Steele until the duration. If you want her, strike a deal with her master."

"I already tried that. He said no."

"Then while she is in his care, there is nothing I can do, short of some grave failing on Steele's part, of course." Cinnamon seethed. His forehead wrinkled and a low growl rumbled from his chest. Hyron laughed.

"I fail to see what's so amusing," he snapped.

"It seems you just might finally know what it's like."

"What's that?"

"To know that there's something your money can't buy."

"Hurry up kid," Steele teased. "The sun's going down. I'd hate for you to be alone in the dark."

"Well we can't all just snap our fingers and conjure sparks, you know," Daphne snapped back.

Steele laughed from his position behind a small boulder. Daphne could see the faint glow of firelight. He was far enough away from her that she couldn't feel any warmth from the flames. The circle of light his fire cast ended about ten feet away. The sun was almost down. Daphne frantically rubbed sticks together. She was wet and shivering and desperate for a tiny spark to start a blaze. After weeks running around in the woods, he'd chosen today to refuse to share a fire with her.

Her body was sore from another day running one of Steele's obstacle courses. He had about 15 different ones hidden throughout the forest and each one ended with a dip in a nearly freezing lake or river. Steele had told her the property they were on belonged to their guild. Daphne would have doubted him if it weren't for the fact that he seemed to know every inch of the grounds. There were times she was sure she'd spotted him walking with his eyes closed and smiling.

Daphne could smell smoke. A tiny spark glinted in the darkness. She looked down and blew gently on the pile of leaves and straw. The tinder caught and the flames grew higher.

"I'm no girl scout, but I'd say—"A sharp pain shot threw her entire body and she fell onto her back as something sharp grazed the side of her head. "Ah!" Daphne screamed. Her shoulder was burning. Daphne's head was spinning. She grabbed her left shoulder. Something long and hard was sticking out of hit. The metal was cold. She could hear footsteps, but she couldn't tell who or what they belonged to.

A hand grabbed her just under her injured arm and began dragging her backward, away from her fire.

"Did you see anything?" Steele asked as he pulled her behind the tiny boulder. He drew a long knife from a hidden pocket behind the seam of his pants leg. He kicked sand onto his fire, quickly smothering the flames. He peered around the boulder at Daphne's still blazing fire. There were no footprints. The only sign that they weren't alone was a small metal arrow lying in the dirt beside Daphne's fire. He listened to the forest, but all he could hear was Daphne whimpering through gritted teeth as she cradled her bleeding shoulder.

"Jesus, this hurts."

"Shhh. I can't hear."

Hot blood oozed around the fingers of her right hand. The pain in her shoulder had intensified. Bright spots flashed in her field of vision. She closed her eyes and leaned her head against the rock. She wiggled her fingers. The action sent a wave of pain shooting into her injured shoulder and the upper part of her back. She carefully ran her fingers along the metal bolt. It was short and smooth. The tip had little prongs on it that simulated feathers.

"Should I pull it out?" she whispered aloud, trying to remember the basic first aid she'd learned in health class.

"Not just yet. I don't have anything to bandage it with."

"I don't care."

"You might once you start to bleed to death."

From what seemed like thin air, he produced a small metal tube. A red laser hummed on. Daphne could feel the heat as Steele held the light near her skin. The acrid smell of hot metal burned her nose as the laser sliced easily through the arrow's thin shaft. A few feet away, sitting just inside the flap of his tent, was the beat up leather backpack that seemed to accompany him whenever he left the house. He waited a few more minutes, listening for any signs of movement in the forest before he retrieved the sack.

He fished a clean sock out of the bag and a shirt. He switched the laser knife to a lower setting and cut the shirt into strips. He pressed the sock against the wound and wrapped it tightly.

"I don't hear anything, let's go."

"Go where?" Daphne asked groggily. He slapped her face and pulled her up by her good arm.

"There's a cabin not too far from here."

"How do you know that?"

"Remember what I told you. These woods belong to our guild. We use them for training. I could walk these woods blindfolded. Come on, stay awake and stay close."

Steele moved slowly. He'd tucked his knife into his belt to allow for faster access. He kept to the thickest parts of the forest to reduce the chances of being followed. He would stop every ten minutes and listen for any sounds in the darkness.

"Hey kid," he whispered. "You still alive?"

"I think I'm gonna be sick," Daphne mumbled.

"It's not much further."

Daphne slipped on a patch of slimy leaves. She bumped against Steele's back. He staggered forward and fell to his knees just moments before the fireball appeared. It whisked past, singeing the ends of their hair.

"Is it just me or is the forest out to get us?"

"Sorry kid, but it looks like your training's officially over. We have to find and kill this son of Vorak."

Daphne retched.

"This is no time for weakness," Steele hissed. "It's either him or us."

Her head hurt and the ground felt like it was bucking beneath her. "What are we supposed to do in the dark? The place…booby trapped?"

"You're probably right," Steele said. "Traps take time to set. Whoever it is has probably been watching us for days."

"Hunter?" she mumbled.

"What?" He could tell she was struggling. To her, the words were probably coming out clearly. Daphne shook her head and rubbed the space between her eyes.

"The woods…your guild, right?"

"Right." He agreed.

The only person who'd know the best place to set a trap would be another member of Realms Honor. If it was a guild member then every normally safe place was a waiting death trap. Steele looked at Daphne. She was on the ground with her back against the trunk of a tree. Her breathing was labored. He touched her face. Her skin was cold and clammy.

Her clothes are still wet from the river, he thought, so it could just be she hasn't had time to dry off and warm up. Of course, he wasn't a doctor, but if he had to guess, that arrow had probably been tipped with some kind of poison. Then again, she could just be suffering from shock.

"Duck," Daphne murmured. Steele dropped to the ground and a cluster of small metal arrows whizzed by. He looked at Daphne in amazement. Normally, she would be completely useless to him. Anyone in her current state would be a burden. Yet, here she was injured and fighting to maintain consciousness and somehow capable of foresight. He slipped her right arm around his shoulders and lifted her to her feet. She even felt lighter than she should've been.

"Which way?" he asked. He could faintly feel the change in the energy around them.

"Go left," she rasped.

Daphne sleepily led them around in a wide circle. She would stop just steps away from a hidden trap and instruct him how to set it off before they continued. By the time they reached their camp, the sunlight was already peeking through the trees. She pushed Steele back and staggered forward.

"Don't move," Daphne slurred. She fell to her knees and crawled to the small rock they'd hidden behind the night before. She used the rock to pull herself up. She sat on top of it and turned her back to the forest. Her eyes were half closed and her body swayed from side to side. To her the forest shimmered. It rippled as though it were a reflection on the surface of a pond on a windy day. There was some sort of light coming off Steele's body. Everything from trees to blades of grass gave off a faint glow.

Steele stiffened his back as a dark shadow slinked from the forest like a fox stealing into a chicken coop. She was dressed in all black. Even the mask she wore obscured her eyes. In her hands was a small knife. Like a ninja, her footsteps were silent. She barely disturbed the dust on the ground as if she'd spent a lifetime walking on rice paper. The stranger's blade glinted in the early light. Steele's body twitched in anticipation. He drew his own knife and dropped into a ready stance.

The woman charged. There was the sound of metal on metal. The force of her attack pushed Steele back. His feet left tracks as he dug his heels into the ground. For the first time since Daphne had known him, Steele's face took on an expression. Instead of the poker face he gave everyone, his eyebrows narrowed. He gritted his teeth and set his jaw. It was obvious that this little figure had more strength and power than her larger opponent.

He parried each of her attacks. He stood his ground, refusing to be pushed back any further. As the next knife swing came, Steele blocked it and dropped to his knees and leaned backward as though he were in a limbo competition. He shoved the fist from his other hand into the woman's stomach and lifted. His opponent was thrown behind him. She landed on her back but quickly regained her feet. They circled each other like hungry wild beasts.

Daphne could smell both of their sweat. The woman was small and fast. Steele was tall and experienced, but he was outmatched. Before long, their attacker's strength and agility was going to get the better of him. If he loses, Daphne thought, I'm as good as dead. Even if they didn't come here for me, I'll be finished.

She shook her head trying to clear the fog that was taking hold. She grabbed the stone for support. Her injured arm was numb. When had that happened? Steele and the ninja were face to face. The woman was standing between Daphne and Steele. Daphne smiled. This woman had written her off as a threat. She'd turned her back on an enemy. Steele gripped his weapon tightly. He was preparing for his final attack. Daphne mouthed the words 'not yet' to him.

Steele didn't allow his expression to change. He shifted his weight from one foot to the other to give the impression that he was preparing to attack.

"Don't think I'd fall for that," the figure hissed. "A hunter always has something up their sleeve." As the woman approached, Steele's mind played through all the possible outcomes. Judging by the outfit, the person before him was a member of the Black Fox Guild. Their knowledge of this isolated section of forest told him they'd belonged to Realms Honor at some point in their career or that they'd been contracted by a member of his own guild to attack him.

The masked figure stopped halfway between Daphne and Steele. She balanced the knife between the knuckles of her right index and middle fingers. In the split second before the knife left her hand, Steele caught the motion of Daphne's lips. He faked as though he were going to try and deflect it and then dodge to the right. Instead, he twitched slightly left and dropped to the ground. The knife passed a hair's breadth from his shoulder. He swept his leg across the ground in an attempt to knock his attacker of balance.

The masked figure danced out of the way. She drew another knife. Steele tried to roll out of the way, but he found he couldn't move. It was as though his body was weighted down. A warm breeze blew over the ground. The woman bounced into the air, gaining momentum for the stabbing blow she was about to deliver. There was the faint sound of a click, like the sound of key in a lock and the Black Fox member collapsed.

She dropped to the ground and lay still. Steele looked at Daphne. A faint orange glow surrounded her. He blinked and the light was gone. She shook his head. It was possible it was just the sun and his fatigue playing tricks on him. Daphne's eyes rolled into the back of her head and she slid sideways off the rock. Her injured shoulder hit the ground first. Steele sat up.

"I'm able to move again." He checked on his enemy. He rolled the individual over with the tip of his foot. There was a tiny metal arrow sticking out of the left eye.

"That was too easy," he said. He looked back at the forest. "Her knife must have hit the lever on a hidden crossbow. It doesn't make sense though," he mused. "A Black Fox would never have missed and sprung their own trap on themselves." He knelt beside Daphne and gently cradled her head in his hands. Her skin was ice cold. She breathed in wheezing gasps.

"Maybe it was a trap for both of you," she said softly.

"Kid, I'll make a hunter of you yet."

Steele's voice fell on deaf ears. Daphne saw his lips move as her eyes slid closed. Her vision exploded with millions of bright lights. After what seemed like hours, the colorful display faded into darkness.

CHAPTER 29

Marcus sat in a chair by the window. He'd been listening to Daphne complain for four days and the past hour had been much of the same. She'd griped about everything. First there was her 30 minute rant on how 36 hours a day was too long to be stuck in a hospital without TV. She'd spent 20 minutes on the number of assignments he'd brought her and now she was going on about the tasteless hospital food. She kept insisting that the addition of a little salt would improve patient morale.

"I quite agree," a nurse said, interrupting Daphne mid-rant. "I got a chance to taste a dish cooked with salt once. It was beyond words."

"See," Daphne said, throwing up her good arm in triumph. "Finally, someone who knows what I'm talking about."

"Unfortunately, you won't get many opportunities to use it as a spice, at least not in the tri-system."

"Why not?"

"What's he teaching you?" she asked. "Even my five year old son knows salt's very rare. There are only a few salt water lakes in the whole tri-system."

"But your planet is huge. And you have two moons that are livable. Don't you have oceans?"

"Of course, but that's all freshwater. Now hold still." The nurse changed the dressing on her shoulder and carefully put Daphne's arm back in a sling. "Don't take it off again," she said sternly.

"Yes ma'am."

"I know it's uncomfortable now but you'll thank me later. Now remember, don't spend all your time flirting with that boy. You have to rest if you're going to heal properly."

Daphne nodded. Marcus watched in amazement as the conversation shifted from medicine to the nurse's personal life. She gushed about her kids and their minor accomplishments. There were ample opportunities for Daphne to whip out a sharp witted remark. Instead, she was uncharacteristically charming. The nurse said her good-bye and notated her patient's chart before leaving to finish her rounds.

"What was that?" he asked his irritation obvious.

"What was what?"

"You give me nothing but sarcasm and attitude. Why me and not her?"

"What can I say? I have a problem with authority."

"Ha. She did nothing but order you around. What happened? Did the poison in that arrow dull the sharpness of your tongue?"

"She has access to drugs that can kill me. Only a moron would be mean to nurses. Besides, I like her. She's working almost every time I come here."

"Just how many times have you been to the hospital?"

"I don't know, a lot."

"You're not suffering from something serious are you?"

"Just a sharp tongue," Steele teased. "But I don't think it's fatal."

"How cute," Daphne said with mock praise. "He thinks he's clever."

Kember laughed as she glided around Steele and set a small wooden box in Daphne's lap. "I hope these will do. I found a jeweler who was throwing out some scraps of palladium. He only charged me for shaping the beads and drilling the holes. Well that and the chain. He wouldn't let me have the beads unless I bought some jewelry."

"Are you kidding?" Daphne said, her eyes wide. "I can't use that. Something like that is way too rare. I'd never be able to pay you back."

"What are you talking about?" Kember asked. Palladium's as common as sand. This whole box is less than 20 brass mercs. The silver chain, now that was a pretty penny."

"What did you want that for anyway?" Steele asked.

"I'm making a rosary."

"A what?" Marcus asked.

"A rosary. They're prayer beads."

"I see," Marcus said. He approached the bed his fascination growing.

"I have something to take care of. I'll see you at the end of the week." Steele planted a kiss on Kember's cheek and left.

Daphne opened the book and fingered the metal beads. There were 53 small beads of a uniform size and 6 larger ones. With his magic, Marcus cut and molded the chain to her specifications. She had one necklace sized chain and hanging from the center was a short piece of chain. Kember helped her feed the beads on in the right order. With her good hand, Daphne slipped her gold cross off her neck. With Marcus' and Kember's help, Daphne removed the clasp and attached it to the silver chain.

"And now, for the finishing touch," she said. She slipped the crucifix off the gold chain and threaded it on the end of the shortest section of chain. She pressed the empty gold chain in Kember's hand. "Is this enough for your trouble?"

Kember smiled and brushed a curl out of Daphne's face and tucked it behind her ear. She placed the thin string of gold in Daphne's hand and folded the girl's fingers around it. "It was no trouble at all."

The guild hall was dark. Hyron had turned most of lights off. Steele didn't need lights to know what the place looked like. The blue marble foyer was emblazoned with a mosaic of a griffin with a five pointed star behind it. On either side of the entrance was a long reception desk. The marble floor deadened at five elevators. The center elevator was the only one that went all the way to the top level. The entire top level not only housed the guild master's office, but his entire living quarters.

At this hour, the only elevator was the one in the middle. The doors stood open. He stepped through the open doors. The elevator began to rise before the doors closed completely. A bell chimed. Steele stood at attention as the elevator came to a stop. The doors slid open. He walked down the hall and into Hyron's office.

The office air smelled unusually fresh. The air was missing the smell of booze and acorn tobacco. Hyron stood in front of his desk. Beside him was a woman with black hair and lavender eyes. She wore a blue and gold dress and held her shoulders erect. The Realms Honor symbol had been affixed to earrings. Hanging from her neck was the emblem of the royal family: a griffin ripping the head off a black dragon. The dragon design was significant because the way it curled around itself made it look more like a black spider.

Steele bowed respectfully, first to the lady and then to his guild master.

"I'd like nothing more than to beat you," Hyron snapped.

"Temper guild master," the woman spoke softly.

"Have I done something wrong?" Steele asked.

"We've received a complaint about the way you treat your apprentice," the woman said.

"May I ask who filed the complaint?"

"No you may not."

"Is my performance under review."

"It is."

"May I ask why?"

Without moving the woman produced a large sheet of paper. She took it in her hand and read it carefully. "Since Daphne has come into your care, she was abused and beaten by Templar guards."

"Allow me to remind your grace that once a prisoner is handed off and payment is received, their wellbeing becomes the responsibility of the Templar."

"While that may be true, it is still your responsibility to check in on your capture and report any corrupt or inhumane activity to the Templar's superiors. Proceeding from there, you then allowed the girl to be held in jail for four days on false charges."

"That was for her own good."

"Did you not fail to promptly retrieve your apprentice or report the actions of the soldiers so they could be held accountable?"

"I did and I apologize. It won't happen again."

"And now I receive a call telling me that you allowed this child to be attacked on realm property."

"We were ambushed. I apologize for my lack of vigilance."

"Not only that, but it seems you failed to remove her from the situation and seek proper medical attention. That doesn't take into account a total of 50 separate hospital visits, half of which resulted in mandatory 72 hour observation. "

"With all due respect, Daphne will recover. She will be released at week's end."

"And the other 50 incidents?"

"All beyond my control. Plant and animal DNA has a tendency to vary from dimension to dimension."

"Had you bothered to concern yourself with the genetic profile submitted by Dr. Ouji, you would have known which plants and animals to avoid. Generally, allowing your apprentice to endure an acceptable level of suffering would not draw my attention. Hardship builds character. However, this girl being here is entirely your fault. It is your responsibility to care for her properly until the portal reopens and you can return her safely to her world."

"I understand."

"Apparently you do not, or I would not be here. You have brought shame to the guild, first by making such an egregious error and then by making such a pitiful show of caring for your foreign charge."

"This performance review is over," Steele said firmly.

"That it is," the lady snapped.

"What is your ruling?"

"Given your previous record, it brings me great displeasure to do this. Unfortunately at present, I must deem you unfit."

"Your grace, I would like to ask for a second chance."

"I'm afraid you passed that mark 30 emergency visits ago. Consider this an official reassignment notice."

"Guild Master—" Hyron held up his hand to silence him. He shook his head. "The mistake was mine. I should never have ordered you to the job. It'd been too long since your last portal jump."

"What's done is done," the woman said. The paper vanished. "Two months Master Hyron, I want a report on my desk in two months. That should give you plenty of time to compile a list with your top three choices for the girl's new master."

"Yes. Of course my lady."

"Once I've given my approval," she said, turning her attention to Steele, "you'll have two weeks to deliver the child to her new master. Is that understood?"

"Yes."

"Tomorrow will begin the standard six month time period, after which the new master's performance must be reviewed. As a favor Steele for the personal service you have shown me in the past, I'll allow her to be transferred back to you after that. Try not to look so browbeaten. She may get transferred back to you before then. It's been my experience that the novelty of a young and cute apprentice wears off after a while."

"Have we concluded our business?" Steele asked.

She nodded. She extended a hand to Hyron. He bowed over it and kissed her ring. Steele bowed and she stepped around him. She walked to the end of the hall, stepped into the elevator and disappeared behind the closing doors.

CHAPTER 30

"That's gin, I think." Dr. Ouji said, spreading twenty matching playing cards on the table.

"I thought you said you stink at this game," Daphne said. She gathered the cards into a pile. Instead of queens, kings, and jacks, the faces of the cards had the images of animals. To her most of them were mythical creatures, but in her studies with Marcus, she'd found that many of the creatures from Earth fairy tales were real here. They just weren't found in the larger than life sizes bedtime stories described.

"It helps when your opponent doesn't know the rules," he laughed. His deep voice reminded her of Sean Connery. She checked to make sure all the cards were facing the same way before sweeping them into a stack. She shuffled the deck four times, cut the deck and shuffled the two halves. She combined them into one big stack and shuffled them again.

"I deal eight, right?" she asked. He nodded. "It's sweet that you came all the way out here to check on me, but you didn't have to you know," she said as she counted out 16 cards. She set the deck in the middle of the dining table and picked up her cards.

"I know I didn't have to, but I wanted to. I don't get out of the office very often and I was overdue for a little vacation time."

"Sitting in a tiny cottage playing cards is your idea of vacation? With faster than light travel I'd think you'd be out there exploring the universe or swimming with space dolphins or something weird like that."

"My dear, when you get to be my age, you find there is wonder in simplicity."

"If you say so," she said, examining her cards. "It's my turn, so I draw six?"

"You're beginning to get the hang of this." There was the sound of a key turning in the lock. "Your master has returned."

"He doesn't usually use the front door. Maybe he's given up on trying to scare me."

The doctor laughed again. "Enjoy the break while you have it. Master's live to make their apprentices miserable. It's the one perk of the job."

Steele looked up in surprise. It was past second moon rise. Kember was usually waiting up for him while Daphne was in bed. Tonight, the roles were reversed. Sitting on the coffee table was a plate covered with a cloth napkin. He closed the door and peeked under the edge of the napkin. Baked chicken and a fruit Daphne referred to as tree potatoes.

"Aren't you allergic to those things?" he asked.

"That's why I put them on your plate." Steele rolled his eyes.

"I brought you something," he said. He sauntered toward the table. In his hand was a fabric package tied with a blue satin ribbon. He set it on the table next to Daphne.

"Does this means we're friends now?" she asked.

"Just open it." He took an empty seat on her right and beckoned the doctor with the fingers of his right hand. Ouji slowly dealt eight cards and slid them left toward the hunter. Daphne gently tugged one end of the ribbon. The bow quickly came undone. She opened the first fold of the fabric. Lying against the dark burgundy material was a Realms Honor pendant.

"Wow. Are you sure you want to give this to me?"

Steele shrugged. "I suppose you earned it."

"I thought I was completely useless."

"Only when you're conscious and in perfect health. But a good master can fix that."

"Guess I'll be useless forever then, huh?" Steele glared as the doctor choked back a laugh. Daphne slipped the rosary off her neck and wrapped it around her wrist like into a layered bracelet. The palladium beads jingled quietly as she slipped the pendant around her neck. Daphne looked at herself in one of the living room mirrors.

"Very cool," she smiled. She unfolded the rest of the material and a small packet of tools clattered to the floor and a bound roll of spandex material bounced onto the table. She hopped down from her chair and retrieved it. "What's this?"

"A few basic tools: lock picks, laser knives. The usual."

She shook out the hooded cloak. The fabric of the cloak was heavy and soft. She ran her fingers against it and let out a whistle.

"Wow. You must really like me. My mom used to sew and I can tell you something like this isn't cheap."

"It's guild standard," Steele muttered. "Are we gonna play or what?"

"Does this outfit have actual hidden pockets like yours or magic ones?" she asked, turning the spandex clothing in her hands.

He rolled his eyes. "Figure it out."

"Can't you give me a little hint?"

"Doctor, I believe it's your turn."

Dr. Ouji chuckled. "I get the feeling the animosity between you two is all surface."

"Yeah right," Daphne scoffed. "He's a jerk."

"And she's a rusty nail in the rear." They were locked in a staring match, each trying to glare the other into submission.

"Whatever you say," the doctor sighed.

Ouji's path was illuminated by the pale glow of the double moons. The light streamed into the hallway from an open bedroom door. That same door had been closed only moments ago when he'd tiptoed to the bathroom. As he passed, he chanced a look inside. The room was slightly larger than his. A twin size bed was pushed against the far left wall. Heavy curtains framed the window, but had been pushed aside to let the moonlight in.

On the windowsill was a picture of a young Daphne with her family. He'd printed it from her mp3 player and framed it for her a few days ago. It was an older picture. In it Daphne appeared to be about 10. Her hair was shorter and pulled into French braid. Her dress was white and decorated with sequins in feathers. In her hands was a small first place trophy. She was centered between her parents. They were kneeling down with their cheeks pressed against hers, their pride was obvious.

On the right was her mother, a woman with suntanned skin and dark auburn hair that curled at the ends. She wore red lipstick and dark purple eye shadow to match her dress. Her green eyes seemed to jump out of the film at him. On Daphne's left, was her father. His dark hair was cut almost to his scalp. His hazel eyes were focused sideways on Daphne's smiling face. His skin was about four shades darker than his daughter's.

Daphne was on the floor beside her bed. She was on her knees with her head bowed. Her curly waist length hair framed her like a wedding veil. Her rosy lips moved silently as her fingers slowly passed over the metal beads she'd been wearing during the card game. She held her hands so close to her mouth that the metal brushed against it. Ouji watched silently as she finished another Hail Mary before shuffling back to the guest room.

As he closed his door, the light in the hall vanished. He heard a soft click as Daphne closed her door. The sound was followed by the sound of someone pounding on a faraway wall. The two thumps were answered by two more, closer this time. There was the faint tapping again and a few seconds later, it was answered. Dr. Ouji waited, but there was silence. He pulled back the covers and slipped into bed. He sighed.

He assumed Steele's tapping on the wall had started out as a simple way to annoy Daphne. She'd responded by answering each of his knocks with ones matching in rhythm. Over time, it had probably become a nightly ritual between the two of them.

"I never would have expected those two to get along," he said to himself. "She should hate him and strike out at him every chance she gets, and yet," he sighed again. It seems I was worried for nothing, he thought. He looked at his watch. If he acted quickly, he could affect the decision. Paying a bribe would tarnish his reputation. It would mean going against his principles and violating his oath as a member of the Lotus Healers, but it was worth it not to have Daphne's life disrupted just as she was starting to find her place.

He fished his phone out of the night table drawer. He dialed one number before it rang.

"Hello?"

"Dr. Ouji?"

"Yes?"

"I have a message for you from Lady Sashabella, royal steward assigned to Realms Honor, and Mystic, regarding the matter of foreign apprentice abuse."

"Yes."

"The situation has been remedied."

"Thank you." The line went dead. Dr. Ouji groaned. He lay with his head on the pillow, listening to the tone. The sound drilled inside his head. He sighed, turned the phone off and tucked it behind his pillow. It was too late. Daphne had been reassigned.

The story continues in…

Other Side of the Wormhole
Book 2: Guild Master Cinnamon